"You pay me, or else you don't leave town."

Jacquie lifted her head in open defiance. "Are you threatening me?"

"I'm promising you," Choya responded evenly.

"How are you going to explain me away?" she challenged. "You don't honestly think people are going to believe I'm only your housekeeper?"

"It doesn't matter what they think." The line of his mouth curved in sardonic amusement. "If anything, people like a man to be a bit of a rogue."

"I simply can't do it." She shook her head hopelessly.

"You don't have any choice," Choya returned with certainty. "It won't really be so bad and it definitely won't last forever.

Janet DAILEY

THE MASTER FIDDLER

Harlequin Books

TORONTO • NEW YORK • LONDON
AMSTERDAM • PARIS • SYDNEY • HAMBURG
STOCKHOLM • ATHENS • TOKYO • MILAN

This edition published January 1993

ISBN 0-373-83230-3

Previously published 1977, 1978, 1979, 1981, 1989

THE MASTER FIDDLER

CHAPTER ONE

AFTER SHE had traveled westward from Dallas, Texas, for two days, the unending desert scenery had begun to bore Jacqueline Grey. The road seemed to stretch through the same land. The rocks and shrubs were jumbled in different order yet appeared almost identical. The heat was oppressive on this September morning.

Actually it was closer to noon, Jacquie realized as the gold bracelets jangled away from the face of her wristwatch. Her start out of Bisbee, Arizona, had not been early, but considering the hour she had gone to bed the night before—or this morning, however one wished to look at it—she deserved congratulations for being behind the wheel at this moment.

With a wry smile curving the fullness of her mouth, she knew that no one mapping out a trip from Dallas to Los Angeles would ever succeed in including Bisbee along its path. Neither would she if it hadn't been for the fact that her girl friend Tammy had recently moved there with her husband.

The sun glared on the road ahead. A dull pain throbbed at Jacquie's temples, an unpleasant reminder of the too many tequila cocktails she had consumed last night. With one hand on the steering wheel, she fumbled through her oversize leather purse for the dusty, rose-shaded sunglasses.

Once in place on the fine bridge of her nose, the glasses shaded her eyes, hiding their unusual turquoise green color without concealing the curling length of her thick lashes. A raking movement of her long fingernails flipped the hair that had fallen across her cheek to the back of her shoulder. The pale, silver gold color of her hair, a completely natural hue since birth, resembled corn silk.

Jacquie was not blind to the somewhat stunning quality of her beauty. Without conceit, she knew the impact she made on the male members of her species when they met her. A beautiful child grown into a beautiful woman of twenty, she was accustomed to second glances and fulsome compliments.

Nor was she the type to falsely bemoan her looks when men concentrated on her physical attributes instead of her intelligence or her vivacious personality. She was attractive and darned glad of it!

As for faults, Jacquie would readily admit to having her share. For starters, she was too much her father's daughter—headstrong, independent, and proud. Secondly, she was spoiled. As an only child of relatively wealthy parents, she had been to a certain extent pampered and indulged. Naturally, she had a temper, a very human trait. Enemies, of which she probably had a few, would be more able to list her failings, Jacquie decided. Except what did all this self-analysis explain, she wondered irritatedly. Certainly not her restless and unsettled mood. It had been with her spasmodically for the last several months. It had brought her here to southern Arizona en route to California.

Last night when she had presented herself at Tammy's doorstep, she had made it sound like a grand adventure, cutting the parental ties and striking out entirely on her own. The argument with her parents, mainly with her father, had been laughingly related.

It hadn't been funny at all. Looking back, Jacquie wished she could take back some of the bitter words she had hurled. Since she hadn't understood the reason for her action, she hadn't been able to explain it to her parents. The argument had begun with her announcement that she wouldn't be returning to the university when the fall term started.

"What do you mean?" her father had demanded, an incredulous frown appearing on his forehead. "You only have two years before you get your degree."

"My degree in what, Dad?" Jacquie had replied somewhat cynically. "I'm a liberal arts major. That means I'm just getting an education in a little bit of everything because I don't know what I want."

"At least you're getting an education. There are a lot of people in this world who would like to trade places with you."

"That's precisely my point." Jacquie had seized on her father's attempt to remind her of the good fortune she had. "There's someone out there who would love to have the education I'm receiving. I don't happen to want it, so I'm quitting to make room for that someone who does."

"How magnanimous of you!" her father had mocked. "And just what do you plan to do instead of attending college?"

"The very same thing I would do after I graduate," she had replied, unable to keep the sarcasm out of her voice. "Get a job."

Her father had impatiently raked his fingers through his hair, now more a silver gray than the silver blond of his daughter's. "Without an education, what type of job do you think you'll get?"

"I don't know. I don't even know what kind I want. An education isn't going to solve that."

"A degree will allow you a wider choice," he had retorted. "Do you know what kind of jobs would be open to you now? I'll tell you. You can be a waitress or a sales clerk or a typist."

"What's wrong with those?" Jacqueline had challenged the faintly snobbish ring of his voice. "They're honest jobs."

"I never said they weren't," he had answered defensively. "Is it wrong for me to want something more for my daughter? At least at college you would be meeting suitable young men."

"The university isn't a marriage market, Dad. And marriage has nothing to do with my decision anyway. I want to be on my own for a while."

"What do you know about earning your own living? You haven't done a day's work in your life!" he had snapped. "It's rare to even see you helping your mother around the house!"

That was the point when the angry words had really begun. Her father's angry accusation that Jacquie only wanted a free ride through life on his shoulders had forced her to insist that she wanted nothing from him but the right to live her own life the way she wanted.

The end result of the argument was this journey to Los Angeles where Jacquie intended to start her new life. There was no particular reason. It had been the first city she had thought of when her father had demanded to know where she was going.

Before she had answered his question, he had bitterly added that he was certain it would be somewhere close by so she could run home to momma when the world got too rough. So the city of Los Angeles had popped out and here she was on her way. It was not the city she would have chosen if she had given it more thought. But once that was said, Jacquie was too stubborn and headstrong to be talked out of her choice.

A glance at the speedometer of her foreign economy car brought an easing of the pressure of her foot against the gas pedal. A chuckle slipped from Jacquie's throat. For two and a half days she had been on her own. Thus far she had acquired a speeding ticket in Texas, another in New Mexico, and a hangover in Bisbee. It was hardly an auspicious beginning.

The roofs of a small town appeared ahead of her. Jacquie had breakfasted only on coffee late that morning, her stomach not prepared for anything more substantial. Now its distinctly hollow feeling might be part of the reason for her dull headache.

There was no curiosity at what small town it might be. Other than verifying which highway would lead her into Tucson, Jacquie had not paid any attention to the route she had plotted that morning, therefore the sign identifying the town limits of Tombstone, Arizona, was unexpected.

Turning the car into the driveway of a service station, Jacquie had the idle thought that after lunching she might wander the boardwalks of the historic western town. The station attendant obligingly gave her directions to the restaurants located on the main street of town only two short blocks from the highway.

More concerned with her immediate destination than any oncoming traffic, Jacquie started to accelerate the car across the road. A horn blared. Her startled gaze swung toward the sound, spying the open-sided jeep an instant before it crunched and bounced off the front side of her car. Neither vehicle had been traveling very fast, but the collision had jolted severely.

Shaken but unhurt, Jacquie tried to open the car door, the image of the little blond-haired boy sitting in the passenger seat of the open jeep filling her mind with terrifying thoughts. The door was jammed. Her futile attempts to open it failed until a superior force from the outside yanked it open.

The dusty rose lenses of her sunglasses shaded, but didn't conceal, the frightened roundness of her eyes. Jacquie stared into the tanned, lean face bending toward her. The man's cheek and jawline were sculptured out of granite, relentlessly hard and grim. His mouth was firmly thinned into a forbidding line. A dusty brown hat was pulled low on his brow and the sunglasses affixed on the aquiline nose revealed only the silvery image of herself.

"Are you all right?" his growling voice demanded.

The accident had lodged her heart in her throat, choking off any words she might have wanted to speak. Jacquie was reduced to nodding dumbly that she was unharmed. There was an ominous tightening of the man's jawline as his face moved away.

On shaking legs, Jacquie forced herself to step out of the car. Her heartbeat had accelerated to a mad pace and her breathing was much too shallow—both aftereffects of the collision, she assured her jangled nerves. She pressed a hand to her throbbing temples before raising her head to gaze at the man standing tall in front of her.

Five foot six in stockinged feet, Jacquie wasn't short by normal standards, but the man dwarfed her. He was easily over six foot with shoulders to fit his height. Perspiration plastered the short-sleeved tan shirt against his chest, the material clinging to the waistband of the dark brown rough cord denims. There wasn't an ounce of spare flesh anywhere.

"You didn't even look for traffic," the man accused in the low voice that reminded Jacquie of thunder rolling toward a crescendo. "Of all the empty-headed, featherbrained—"

The rest was bit off in mid sentence as the barely imperceptible movement of his head indicated a shift of his attention. Jacquie glanced hesitantly over her shoulder. The little blond boy she had fleetingly glimpsed in the jeep was hobbling toward them on crutches, his right leg in a plaster cast.

Rounded eyes of the palest brown were riveted on Jacquie. "Are you all right?" the boy inquired anxiously.

Her voice returned in a sighing laugh as her mouth curved into a tremulous smile. "Scared out of my wits," she admitted, "but I'm not hurt."

"I thought I told you to stay in the jeep, Robbie."

The boy's eyes flickered to the man beside Jacquie, then skittered to the rocky ground near his feet, his chin tucked against his chest. "Yessir," the boy named Robbie admitted.

The boy's concern had been genuine and Jacquie couldn't stop herself from softening the rather harsh attitude of his father. The return of her voice had brought a return of her poise and strength. Ignoring the man beside her, she walked the few steps to the boy.

"Are you all right?" she asked gently, pushing her sunglasses on top of her silvery blond head and bending toward him.

He peered at her through stubby brown lashes, his gaze locking with fascination on the long hair that swung forward across her cheeks. "Yes ma'am."

"I'm glad," Jacquie smiled.

"Your hair is pretty," he breathed absently.

Her eyes darted to the tow-headed shade of his hair. "It's almost the same color as yours," she pointed out.

The small, thin fingers of his right hand, the arm resting on the crook of his crutch, started forward as if to touch the spun silver gold of her hair, but the man's voice arrested the boy's movement.

"Wait for me at the station with Bob, Robbie," the man ordered crisply.

The chin lowered again. "Yessir," the boy mumbled the words together. His small hands tightened on the crutches to propel him forward. A hesitant smile was offered to Jacquie. "I'm glad you're all right."

"So am I." Jacquie straightened and watched the boy's awkward progress toward the service station.

The man's broad shoulders blocked her vision after the boy had traveled several feet. Harsh displeasure was etched in the thin line of his mouth. With her usual aplomb, Jacquie smiled warmly.

"An apology isn't sufficient, I know, but I truly am sorry about the accident. I'm not usually so careless," she offered.

The mirroring sunglasses prevented her from seeing his eyes, yet she couldn't shake the sensation that his piercing gaze had just raked her curving figure, taking note of the snug fit of her cranberry slacks, the bare skin of her middle revealed by the midriffed top of clinging knit. Not one flicker of admiration appeared in any way on the man's carved features.

Jacquie's assessment of him had been that he was all man, but he had evidently found her wanting in some respect. It was vaguely irritating that he had failed to respond to the warmness of her smile.

"At least you recognize you were careless," he murmured cynically, a faint curl to his upper lip.

Counting to ten, Jacquie turned away from him. It was never wise to lose your temper when you were in the wrong. "How badly did I damage your jeep?" she asked instead.

"A dented bumper, no worse than that," the man answered, a mocking inflection in his tone. "It's made to take punishment. The same can't be said for yours."

A glance at the crumpled bumper of the jeep affirmed his words a second before he mentioned her car. Jacquie pivoted around, dismay pulling down the corners of her mouth when she saw the mashed front end of her little car.

"You're lucky it wasn't worse," the man stated, leaving unspoken his implication that he thought she deserved worse. "The police will be here shortly to make out a report, then Bob—" nodding the crown of his brown Stetson toward the service station "—can give you some idea of the extent of the damage."

"The police," Jacquie repeated weakly, thinking with dread of the two speeding tickets she had already paid and the undoubted citation she would receive as the driver in error at this accident.

What with fines and the repairs to the car, her supply of cash wasn't going to be as large as she thought by the time she reached Los Angeles.

"Yes, the police," he spoke the words again with biting conciseness.

"There . . . there really isn't any need to involve them in this," she began hopefully, blinking her sea-green eyes at him and receiving no outward reaction to her appeal. "I mean, after all, the damage was mostly to my car. No one was hurt, so why bother them?"

"There was an accident involving considerable property damage. It has to be reported." His commanding voice left no room for argument.

"I see," Jacquie nodded, pretending her previous request had been made in ignorance of the law.

At about that time, a car, bearing an official insignia on its door, pulled into the service station behind them. It was just as well that Jacquie hadn't argued the point.

The officer greeted Robbie's father with easy friendliness. The actual questioning period was brief, due mainly to the clear, concise account of the accident given by the tall, imposing man. The officer took one look at Jacquie, who couldn't be expected to be totally perfect in everything. Had it not been Robbie's father but some other man susceptible to her attraction involved in the accident Jacquie believed she could have avoided the citation for reckless driving. But the man's presence seemed to demand that she be issued it.

Within seconds after the paper was in her hand, another was thrust toward her by sun-browned fingers. Before she had an opportunity to read the writing scrawled on the plain paper, the man informed her that it was the name and address of his insurance company and could he please have hers—a command phrased in a politely worded request that grated.

Rumaging through her oversized purse, Jacquie found paper and a pencil and quickly wrote down the information. He shoved it in his shirt after a verifying glance at what was written.

"Good day," the man said crisply, more to the officer than Jacquie.

Without a backward glance, his long strides carried him to the jeep where his long legs were tucked under the wheel. She watched with faint anger while he pulled into the nearby service station to collect Robbie, wishing that she had given in to the sarcastic impulse to tell him it had been nice running into him.

From the passenger seat of the open-sided jeep, a small hand waved goodbye. Jacquie returned the gesture with a determined flourish of her arm, wondering how a sensitive little boy could have such an insensitive father. With the very willing assistance of the officer and the service-station attendant, her car, no longer able to move under its own power, was towed the few yards to the garage. A sigh was expelled as she wondered how extensive the damage might be.

"How long do you think it will take?" Bracelets jangled as she tucked silken hair behind her ear, her eyes anxiously studying the mechanic's face after his initial inspection of the damage.

"Can't tell," he shrugged. "A while, I expect. Providing I can get the parts I need. That's a foreign-made car you got."

"Yes," Jacquie sighed, fearing the worst at this moment.

"You'll want me to give you an estimate first before I go ahead and start fixin' it, won't you?" he inquired, tilting a cap back on his receding hairline and wiping the grease from his hands on a rag.

"Of course," she nodded, but she knew it was only a business formality. She really had little choice except to let him fix it, regardless of how badly it depleted her cash reserve. Glancing down at her hands, she noticed the piece of paper twisted in her fingers. Unfolding it, she read the precise handwriting and spoke the name out loud.

"Choya Barnett." A frown creased her forehead. "Choya," she repeated it. "What kind of a name is that?"

"What?" the mechanic looked at her blankly.

"Choya," Jacquie tried the name out again and the man's blank expression didn't change. "The man I ran into—his name."

A chuckle of understanding broke from the mechanic's lips. "It's pronounced cho-yä. Choya Barnett."

Jacquie murmured the correct pronunciation, finding it easier and more musical. Then she shook her head. "I've still never heard it before."

"It comes from a kind of cactus in the prickly-pear family," the man explained with a smile.

"I beg your pardon?" She tilted her head to the side.

"The cholla cactus, spelled c-h-o-l-l-a, but pronounced cho-yä," the mechanic repeated. "Choya Barnett was named after that cactus. Old man Barnett found him in a bed of cholla when he was a baby. Barnett spelled it the way it sounded."

A bubble of laughter rose in her throat. Jacquie bit hard on her lower lip, reducing it to a silent giggle. How appropriate! He was named after a thorny cactus! The more she thought about the name, the better it suited him. Its meaning was appropriate and the sound of it was proud, like the man.

"If you want to go eat, miss, while I get this written up," the mechanic suggested, "you're welcome to go ahead. I'm going to have to make a few phone calls anyway to get some prices on parts I'll need."

"Yes, I think I will," Jacquie agreed, still smiling at her secret thoughts and inner laughter.

The sunglasses resting on top of her head were pushed onto her nose as she gathered up her purse and walked out the station door. At least there was some saving humor to the situation.

Crossing the highway, Jacquie chose the shaded side of the street, seeking relief from the blazing sun overhead. On Allen Street she quickly sought the air-conditioned coolness of the closest restaurant. The lunch hour crowd had nearly filled the restaurant and there was only one vacant booth and one table in the place. She seated herself at the booth, accepting the menu the waitress brought. She paid no attention to the opening of the restaurant door until she heard the clumping sound of a pair of crutches.

A glance at the door met the partly shy smile of Robbie Barnett. He was making his way determinedly toward her booth, or more correctly the empty table diagonally across from Jacquie.

"Hello," the boy offered.

"Hello again," Jacquie responded. Her wide smile made the pale brown eyes glow with pleasure. A darted look behind the boy noted that Choya Barnett had been detained near the door by another customer. "Are you going to have lunch, too?"

"Yes, ma'am," Robbie nodded politely, glancing almost with longing at the vacant booth seat opposite Jacquie. It was on the tip of her tongue to invite him to sit with her, but she knew the invitation would not be welcomed by his father.

In silence, she let him continue his way to the table. Yet her gaze remained on the small, blond-haired boy, irresistibly drawn to him perhaps by some latent maternal instinct she hadn't been aware of possessing.

Balanced on his crutches, he pulled out a chair and maneuvered himself and the unwieldy cast on his right leg in front of it. The boy was small and the chair was large. He sat on the edge of the chair seat, legs dangling, the cast looking awkward and heavy.

Rising to her feet, Jacquie crossed the short space to the table. Her fingers closed over the back of the chair next to Robbie Barnett and slid it closer to his.

"I think you would be more comfortable if we rested your leg on the seat of this chair," she suggested brightly, uncaring whether the boy's welfare was any of her concern or not.

Helping him to slide back in the seat, she positioned the second chair to serve as a leg rest and lifted his plastered leg onto it.

"How's that, Robbie?" she asked.

"Fine," he nodded, a shy smile curving his mouth as he again peered at her through the tops of his spiky lashes.

"My name is Jacquie," she said, offering her hand as she made the introduction.

"That's a boy's name," he frowned while he very seriously shook her hand.

"It's short for Jacqueline," she explained.

"Like mine is long for Rob," he nodded with understanding. "I'm seven, almost."

"I'm considerably older than that, closer to twenty-one," Jacquie smiled, remaining in a slightly bent position.

"My dad's older than that," Robbie replied with a faint shrug of his small shoulders, as if she didn't need to apologize for being so old.

"Excuse me, Miss Grey," a cool voice said behind Jacquie. Its low, controlled tone left her in no doubt it belonged to Choya Barnett, even before she turned. "Don't you think my son is rather young for you to be flirting with him?"

Jacquie straightened with a pivot, bringing the full brilliance of her blue green eyes to bear on him. The dusty Stetson hat and mirrorlike sunglasses had been discarded. His dark, umber brown hair grew with thick carelessness away from the wide, tanned forehead.

But his eyes were a surprise. They were a strange shade of tawny gold. The gold flecks belonged to a more dangerously predatory beast like the cougar. They were watching her now with the suggestion of coiled alertness, ready to spring without warning. An antagonistic feeling stirred within Jacquie, making her thrust her pointed chin forward.

"Would you prefer, Mr. Barnett, that I choose someone more your age?" she asked in an icily composed tone.

The strong male mouth quirked crookedly at her question. The tawny eyes flicked downward to the knit material molding the full, rounded curve of her breasts.

"I am sure you could be quite diverting," he replied, watchfully holding her flittering eyes, "but there are others who would welcome you more than I."

He was being deliberately insulting. Her blood heated to a slow boil. Jacquie sensed that he resented her intrusion into his life and was determined she should be aware of it.

"How refreshing it is to discover fidelity in a man in this day and age," she murmured, instead of voicing the angry retort that had formed in her throat. "Your wife must be very happy."

"Yes," he agreed smoothly, and stepped around her, dismissing her as effectively as if he had told her to get lost.

Short of standing there looking lost and snubbed, she had little choice but to return to her booth seat. *Choya, a cactus,* she thought to cool her growing temper. *Prickly on the outside to keep anyone from coming too close. What was he like on the inside?*

One thing was certain, Jacquie decided as she picked up the menu again; Choya Barnett didn't seem to care for attractive blondes. At least, he had made it plain that she didn't affect him at all.

If that's the way he wanted it, then she would simply ignore him, too.

CHAPTER TWO

CHOYA BARNETT was not a man to ignore. He exuded a presence that could be felt even when Jacquie was not looking at him. No matter how she tried not to let him dominate her consciousness during the luncheon meal, he did.

Masculine and virile, he was handsome with a dangerous kind of fascination about him because of the ruggedness of his features. The tawny gold eyes seemed to never reflect anything of what he was thinking. Eyes were supposed to be mirrors of the soul. Didn't he have a soul?

Robbie had to take after his mother. The pale brown eyes were the only thing about the small boy that was reminiscent of his father. Jacquie found herself wondering what kind of a woman his wife was. Sensitive like her son? Poor woman, was the immediate reaction to that thought. Choya Barnett would ruthlessly walk over any weak-willed individual. His wife had better have a very strong backbone or she would turn into a hollow shell of her husband's molding.

Maybe that was why he didn't like Jacquie, because she stood up to him and he knew it. Not that it mattered, she reminded herself, when the man and his son had finished their meal and left. As soon as her car was repaired, she would be leaving.

The mechanic gave her the unpromising advice—when she returned to the station after lunch—that she should take a walk around town and see some of the sights. He informed her that certainly her car wouldn't be repaired before five that afternoon. Since it was Saturday, he warned her that it was a good chance that he wouldn't be able to obtain the needed parts.

Jacquie refused to think about the last possibility—that she would be in town over the weekend. Who would have thought that her side trip to Bisbee would have landed her in this mess with her car broken down? She should have driven straight through to Los Angeles with no social visits in between. Hindsight always was a wiser view.

Luckily there were plenty of places to visit in the old historic town, museums with relics of the town's wild West past and gift shops. She considered booking a room in one of the motels, but was afraid such negative thinking would automatically keep her in Tombstone over the weekend.

And she toyed with the idea of telephoning Tammy in Bisbee if the worst should occur and she had to stay until Monday. But she decided against that—just why she wasn't certain. She had enjoyed the visit to her girlfriend. Maybe she subconsciously wanted the solitude of a couple of days spent alone. She would certainly have time to formulate more definite plans to be enacted when she arrived in Los Angeles.

Along about four o'clock, she wandered slowly through the streets making her way in the general direction of the service station. The shady trees of the small town park beckoned her and she obeyed their invitation to sit on one of the benches beneath their limbs. Truthfully Jacquie didn't see the small blond boy in the far section of the park. In fact, she didn't even notice him until he came toward her bench.

"Robbie!" she said with genuine surprise. "Hello, I didn't expect to see you again. I thought you had probably gone home."

"Not yet." He shook his head, a pleased grin splitting his thin face at her immediately welcoming smile. "My dad will be coming to get me pretty soon, though."

Just when she had succeeded in pushing Choya Barnett to the back of her mind, his image cropped up again. She inwardly shrugged away the disturbing picture.

"Where do you live? Here in Tombstone?" she asked.

"On a ranch in the Dragoon Mountains." His tongue drawled out the word "dragoon" with slight difficulty.

"I see, and your father had business in town today," Jacquie responded. "Do you like living on a ranch?"

"Most of the time it's a lot of fun," he informed her earnestly. "'Cept now, since I broke my leg. There isn't as much to do."

"Do you have any brothers or sisters?"

"No, there's just me and Gramps and Dad," Robbie answered simply.

"And your mother, of course." Jacquie was suddenly aware that she was subconsciously prying information out of him, but she was too curious to stop herself.

The small face became suddenly masked and uncommunicative. "No."

"No?" Jacquie spoke unconsciously, because her mind was suddenly racing with possibilities. Did that mean his mother was alive or dead? If she was alive, had her departure been recent? Was she separated from Choya Barnett or divorced? Why had she left her child?

The shuffling of the boy's crutches brought her attention swiftly back to him. His face was hidden by a downcast chin, the white-blond of his hair shimmering with silky fineness. As if feeling her gaze, Robbie Barnett slowly raised his head, giving her a long considering look.

"My mother died when I was little," he said, putting an end to her unanswered questions. "I don't remember her."

For all the calmness of his voice, there was a touching wistfulness in his eyes. The faint sadness was transmitted to Jacquie. It was not his mother's death the boy mourned as much as the fact that he didn't remember her. Reaching out, her fingers touched the lightly tanned smoothness of his cheek.

"I'm sorry, Robbie," she murmured and she meant it.

He stared at her for a long moment, not moving. When she withdrew her hand from his cheek, his gaze shifted to her fingers. Jacquie wanted to say something, to ask what was wrong, but she couldn't.

Finally Robbie broke the silence, turning a pair of earnest brown eyes to her face. "Daddy lets me keep her picture in my room. She was very pretty."

"I'm sure she was," Jacquie nodded quietly.

"You look a lot like her. Your hair is the same color and everything," he declared fervently.

Smiling, Jacquie understood now why the boy seemed to have been drawn to her almost from the beginning. He had been fascinated by the silver gold color of her hair when he had first seen her after the accident. Admittedly it was not a shade often seen.

"That's a very nice compliment to give a girl, Robbie," she responded, "especially when you've already told me that your mother was a very pretty woman. Thank you."

His statement brought up another interesting possibility. If she did resemble his mother, could it be the reason Choya Barnett had been so abrupt with her? Did he look at Jacquie, too, as the ghost of his dead wife come back to haunt him? It would certainly explain his chilling attitude toward her.

Light brown brows were drawn together as Robbie studied her again. "Are you married, Jacquie?" he asked.

"No, not me," she laughed shortly and with easy humor. "I'm not ready to be tied down yet."

"Aren't you staying in Tombstone?" He tipped his head to one side in confusion.

"Only as long as it takes to have my car fixed," she told him. Adopting a teasing western drawl, she added, "Just passin' through, podner. Which reminds me," Jacquie glanced at her wristwatch, surprised to discover it was nearly five o'clock. "I'm supposed to be at the station by five. It's nearly that now."

"I wish you didn't have to go," Robbie mumbled, the corners of his mouth drooping.

In a way, Jacquie wished she didn't have to go, too. Then she scolded herself for being so sentimental. He was a little boy, not much different from any other little boy. It was silly to feel so attached to him when, once her car was repaired, she would never see him again.

She quickly gathered her bag from the bench seat and stood up. Robbie stood in mute silence, watching her movements yet not looking up into her face.

Solemnly, Jacquie offered him her hand in farewell. "Goodbye, Robbie. Your father will probably be here shortly to take you home anyway."

"'Bye," he answered gruffly, briefly touching her hand before he used his crutches to turn himself around to retreat the way he had come.

Jacquie stared at the crestfallen figure hopping away, a ridiculous lump rising in her throat. A strong impulse took hold of her to forget about the time and her car and wait with this little boy until his father came to get him.

But a few more minutes together wouldn't make the parting any easier.

Resolutely squaring her shoulders, Jacquie turned away toward the street sidewalk. There, previously unnoticed by either Jacquie or Robbie, stood his father—for how long, Jacquie could only guess. Something inside said that it couldn't have been long or she would have felt him even if she hadn't seen him.

"Hello," she spoke quickly, trying to shake the sensation that she had been caught doing something she shouldn't.

The only acknowledgment of her greeting was a curt nod of the dusty-brimmed Stetson. The mirrorlike sunglasses were again shading his eyes, but Jacquie knew the cat-gold gaze was studying her relentlessly. He started forward, long legs carrying him with supple ease.

Jacquie turned her head in the direction that Robbie had taken, but her gaze never strayed from Choya Barnett.

"Robbie," she called smoothly, but with every nerve tensely alert, "your father is here. I told you he wouldn't be long."

A whispering breeze stirred her hair, and she brushed a hand across her cheek as if pushing away an imaginary lock of hair. It gave her the seconds of composure she needed. For some unknown reason, she felt she needed to explain the reason she had been with Robbie.

"I was on my way to the garage to see if my car had been repaired. I stopped in the park here to get out of the sun for a while and found Robbie," she offered.

"Your car isn't repaired yet?" Choya Barnett had reached her side, or as close as he was going to come, stopping a good five feet from her to wait for the necessarily slow approach of his son.

"I hope so," Jacquie smiled, trying to deny the tingling sensation of unease. "But the mechanic warned me that there might be some difficulties getting the right parts. My car is one of those imported economy models, unfortunately."

His expression, that part that wasn't concealed by dark sunglasses, only indicated boredom with her explanation. As soon as she had finished speaking, the strong chin tilted downward toward the boy, pausing in front of him, closer to Jacquie than to his father.

"Are you ready to leave, son? Gramps will probably be waiting dinner." It was hardly a question. The man had politely worded it as such, but it was clear he expected no other answer except agreement.

"Yes, sir." Robbie voiced the anticipated agreement, but without enthusiasm. The light brown eyes swept upward to Jacquie's face, mutely reluctant to leave her.

"Goodbye again, Robbie." She intended the words to come bright and gay, but they were oddly taut.

"Miss Grey." Choya Barnett's voice slashed out sharply, cutting away the vague sense of intimacy that Robbie's searching gaze had enveloped her in. Her gaze of turquoise green swung to the carved male features, imposingly rugged and powerful. "The garage is on the way to my ranch. I'll give you a ride there."

It was hardly more than two blocks that Jacquie had to walk to reach the garage. The command—it certainly wasn't an invitation— didn't seem to make much sense until she noticed the beaming smile of gratitude and adoration that radiated over Robbie's face as he gazed at his father.

The man's heart wasn't totally made of stone, she decided. Not if he was willing to put up with her obviously unwelcome company for two blocks in order to please his son.

A speculating light entered her eyes. "That's thoughtful of you, Mr. Barnett. Thank you," she said in acceptance of his offer, and wondered why that sardonic line had tilted the firm male mouth.

"My jeep is parked at the curb," he said.

Falling into step with Robbie, Jacquie followed the wide shoulders of Choya Barnett to the street, his long strides leading the way.

There was a suggestion of impatience in his erect carriage, as if he regretted the invitation to give her a lift to the garage. He paused beside the passenger side of the jeep, turning to watch their progress through the concealing darkness of his sunglasses. "The back is cluttered and dusty," he stated crisply. "The two of you should be able to share the front seat without too much difficulty for the short distance to the garage."

"I'm sure we can," Jacquie agreed, glancing down at the boy hesitating beside her.

"Hand me your crutches, Robbie." Lean brown fingers reached out for the first crutch, shifting it to the other hand while he waited for Robbie to balance himself against the jeep before giving up the second. With the crutches stowed behind the seat, Choya picked up the boy, carefully lifting him into the front seat. As Jacquie moved to join Robbie, cool fingers gripped her elbow to assist her into the small portion of the shared seat.

Her "thank you" for his help was spoken into empty air. The tall figure was already walking around the front of the jeep. With an economy of movement, Choya Barnett swung himself behind the wheel, long legs smoothly fitting in the confined area. The motor was switched on and they were driving away.

Ignored by the strong, masculine profile, Jacquie turned her attention to the small boy nestled against her shoulder. His expression was one of definite pleasure in the situation.

"You never did tell me how you broke your leg, Robbie," she said as the motion of the jeep generated a breeze that tangled her corn silk hair around her face.

"I got bucked off a bull." His mouth twisted into a reluctant grimace, followed by a self-conscious glance at his father.

"A bull?" Jacquie repeated in disbelief.

"I'm going to ride in the rodeo when I grow up," he informed her importantly. "Gramps said you should start learning when you're young."

A frown of disbelief remained implanted on her forehead as she studied the small, blond head beside her. "You don't mean you actually tried to ride a bull?"

"Robbie." The male voice was low and carried a vague warning in its tone, although the man's attention didn't leave the road.

There was an instant of silence. Then small shoulders moved in a speaking shrug. "Well, it was actually a bull calf," Robbie admitted. "I'm not big enough to ride a real bull yet."

"I should hope not!" Jacquie laughed shortly. Then she glanced curiously at the driver. "Do you ride in the rodeo, Mr. Barnett?"

"No," he replied without any further elaboration to encourage the conversation.

"I see," she responded, refusing to give up. "I thought perhaps Robbie was mimicking you—like father, like son."

"It was entirely his idea." This time the strong jaw turned, tilting downward toward the boy. "Wasn't it, Robbie?"

Again Choya Barnett's voice was prodding. It evidently found its target as a faint flush crept into the boy's cheeks.

"Yes, sir," Robbie murmured guiltily. "And I won't try it again unless you or Gramps are there."

That revealing statement completed the sketchy description of the accident for Jacquie. She had wondered why Choya Barnett had been so determined not to allow the boy to brag about his injury. Robbie was too young to realize the danger in his obviously unsupervised attempt to ride a calf. The broken leg hadn't seemed to instill any sense of caution either, she decided thoughtfully.

The jeep was slowed and turned into the driveway of the service station where her car had been left. The mechanic was standing in the open arch of the overhead garage doors. He walked forward at the jeep's approach. "Sorry, miss," he said before Jacquie could slip from the passenger seat, "but I wasn't able to get those parts I needed from Tucson. I can't have your car repaired now before Monday afternoon some time."

"Oh, no!" Even though he had warned her of this possibility, the grumbling protest came automatically in a sigh.

"I'm sorry," the mechanic repeated with a philosophical smile.

"I quite understand that you can't help it," she grimaced, glancing down the highway toward the motel sign. "I'll just have to find a place to spend the night, that's all."

"There are a couple of nice places to stay here. The motel down the road still has a vacancy sign," the man suggested.

One place was as good as another, Jacquie decided. "Thanks for the lift, Mr. Barnett," she offered as she stepped out of the jeep.

"Jacquie—" Robbie began eagerly.

But his father broke in abruptly. "If you want to get your things from your car, Miss Grey, I'll take you on to the motel now."

The offer surprised her, more so than the lift to the garage. A brow raised faintly, before she nodded agreement.

"Thank you. I appreciate that."

Her car was parked inside the garage, well within view of the jeep in the drive. As she gathered her overnight bag and cosmetic case from the rear of her car, Jacquie glimpsed the somewhat intense discussion going on between father and son. Judging by the faintly sulky expression on Robbie's face when she returned, the conclusion had not been in his favor.

"Do you have everything you need?" Choya Barnett inquired politely, but in a cuttingly indifferent tone.

"Yes, thank you," Jacquie nodded, feeling somehow that she shouldn't have accepted the offer.

The man was a definite puzzle, offering her a ride when he so obviously wanted to be rid of her. There was little doubt that she had been the subject under discussion. The reason escaped her.

If Choya Barnett wanted to separate her from his son, then why was he prolonging the time she spent in his son's company? Or had the offer been a means of interrupting Robbie before he said something that his father would not approve? That seemed likely.

Sliding onto the seat with Robbie, Jacquie balanced the cases on her lap, taking care they didn't bump the plaster cast on his leg as Choya Barnett shifted the jeep into forward gear. A covert sideways glance studied the carved profile, the lean angular jaw and the firm mouth, impassive in its expression.

Face it, Jacquie smiled wryly to herself, you're fascinated with the man. He's quite unlike anyone you've ever met and you'd like to know what makes him tick, she told herself. The very fact that he's not overwhelmed by your looks just makes him all the more intriguing. It would be less than honest not to admit that she found him something of a challenge.

When Choya Barnett stopped the car in front of the motel, Jacquie fully expected him to let her out and leave immediately. Before she could offer him her thanks again, he was switching the motor off and stepping out of the jeep to walk around to her side. She guessed the widening of her aquamarine eyes revealed her surprise.

Nothing in his expression told her anything. The impassive features made it impossible for her to determine whether he was doing it out of politeness or a desire to make certain he was definitely rid of her.

The larger overnight bag was taken from her. "I'll carry this in for you," he stated in a tone that didn't allow any argument.

Jacquie gave it up silently, swinging her feet onto the ground to stand beside him. Curiosity overpowered her as she stared into the blankness of his sunglasses.

"Why are you doing this, Mr. Barnett?"

"Doing what?" His head drew back slightly, arrogance in the set of his jaw that his action should be questioned. "I'm merely trying to be hospitable to a stranger who's found herself stranded in our town."

"Really?" she returned with challenging doubt.

"What else do you think it would be, Miss Grey?" He stepped to the side, indicating that she should precede him to the motel lobby.

"I'm not sure," she murmured as she started toward the door.

Inside the motel, Choya introduced her to the proprietress, explaining the circumstances leading to Jacquie's need for the room, but omitting to say that he had been the second party in the accident. The woman displayed no surprise whatever that Choya Barnett had deputized himself to see that Jacquie found accommodation for the weekend.

In record time she had signed the register and been issued a key to her motel room. Having already been snubbed once for asking the reason for his seeming solicitude, Jacquie didn't risk it again as she led the way to her motel room with Choya following behind with her overnight case. The sunglasses had been removed in the relative dimness of the building after the glare of the outside and were tucked in his shirt pocket. But the tawny cat eyes told her no more of the reason for his aid than his expression did.

Unlocking the motel room door, she swung it open for his entry first. Without a word he

stepped by her into the room, flicking on the
switch for the overhead light. Jacquie started
to follow him into the room, bending her head
to hide the smile that swept across her face as
she suddenly wondered what he would do if
she tried to pay him for his assistance. He
would not find it amusing, she knew.

The toe of her sandal shoe hooked the edge
of the throw rug inside the door. She was
thrown forward, handbag and cosmetic bag
were dropped as her arms reached out to break
the fall.

But the expected sprawl onto the floor never
happened. With the reflex action of one accustomed to reaching swiftly, Choya Barnett
stepped forward, catching her before she
ended up in a heap. One minute Jacquie was
falling forward and in the next an iron band
was around her waist, abruptly checking her
movement and drawing her upright in one
motion. Her weight seemed feather light to
him.

Gasping her surprise at the fall that hadn't
occurred, she felt her heart start beating again.
Her hands were resting weakly against a hard
wall. With difficulty she focused her eyes on it
and discovered the white collar of his shirt
opened at the throat to reveal the deep tan of
his chest. Then she became aware of the iron

grip of his arms, tightly surrounding her and holding her firmly against him.

Tipping back her head, pale gold hair cascading over her shoulders, she gazed into his face, that ruggedly masculine face only inches from her own. The amber flame in his eyes seemed to catch at her breath as it burned over her features. The impulse to kiss him was automatic and instinctive, leaping from some hidden inner source that she couldn't explain.

Inexorably, she let her lips move closer to the harsh line of his male mouth. His head dipped toward her in response to her invitation and the fiery warmth of his mouth closed over hers, hardening to deepen the kiss. Before the action was carried out, she was thrust angrily away, held firmly at arm's length for another second before she was released completely from his touch.

Her lips were still parted in anticipation of the scorching kiss that had been doused before it had ignited. She blinked in disbelief at the unemotional gold-flecked eyes that gazed at her so coolly now.

"You aren't as indifferent to me as you'd like to pretend, are you, Mr. Barnett?" she accused in a low and breathless voice.

"I'm a man," he stated coldly as if at this moment she had any doubt about it. "It was an unconscious reaction. I promise I don't intend to make that mistake again.''

She shook her head, unable to understand what she was hearing. ''Why...why don't you like me? What have I done?'' Fingers trembled across her forehead, continuing their path to smooth the hair away from her face. ''It can't be because of the accident?''

His mouth thinned with sardonic amusement. ''Not that alone,'' Choya Barnett agreed. ''But you are trouble, spelled with capital letters, and that makes you one thing I definitely don't need.''

''Then why did you take the time to bring me to the hotel?'' she demanded, a faint anger growing that she should be so unjustly labeled. ''I never believed it was Western hospitality!''

''When there's trouble, I like to know where it is. Does that answer your question, Miss Grey?'' A slashing dark eyebrow arched in arrogant inquiry.

Jacquie averted her head. ''Yes, it does, very adequately. I hope you understand if I don't thank you for all you've done,'' she snapped sarcastically.

She was fast losing her temper. Invariably when she became angrily emotional, tears would start to fall. She wanted Choya Barnett gone before she lost control of her temper.

"I understand," he replied with dry cynicism, "very well."

Her hands doubled into fists as the motel door closed behind him. She picked up the cosmetic bag and handbag she had tossed onto the floor prior to her near fall, and in a fit of rage, she hurled them onto the bed, wishing she had thrown them at him instead. How he must be laughing at the way she had invited him to kiss her! She had never been so degradingly rejected in all her life. Trouble! He didn't know the meaning of the word!

CHAPTER THREE

THE SHARP rocks seemed to penetrate the thin soles of her sandals, jabbing the sensitive bottom of her feet until Jacquie was reduced to picking her way alongside of the road. Although it wasn't yet midmorning, the sun was already beginning to make its strength felt with searing rays.

When she had started out a few minutes before, it had seemed logical to walk the short distance to the famous Boothill Cemetery. But not daring to walk on the busy highway, Jacquie had been forced to walk on the uneven gravel of the road's shoulder. After the first few jagged edges of the sharp gravel had dug into her soles, she had not taken her attention from the ground. A horn blared behind her, signaling an approaching vehicle.

"Oh, go jump in a lake!" she grumbled, exclaiming sharply as she hopped away, nearly turning her ankle on an oversized chunk of stone.

The vehicle that honked didn't whizz by as others had done. Instead it pulled to a stop beside her. The cutting words that had been forming to check any invitation from a stranger died in her throat as Jacquie recognized the jeep beside her and the imposing man behind the wheel.

"Are you leaving town, Miss Grey?" Choya Barnett inquired mockingly. He wasn't wearing sunglasses and the lazy, tawny-colored eyes seemed to find her discomfort amusing.

"Not on foot," she snapped harshly. She hadn't slept at all well last night, tossing and turning until well after midnight, and she blamed her sleeplessness more on the man she faced now than on the fact that she had been trying to sleep in a strange bed. "What are you doing in town this morning? Checking to see where 'trouble' was?" Her voice was sarcastic.

He ignored that. "If you intend to walk far, you really should have some substantial type of shoes on your feet, not those paper-thin pieces of leather."

"Thanks for the advice. I figured that out for myself, though." Jacquie started walking again, determined to snub the man the way he had snubbed her.

The jeep rolled slowly along to keep him abreast of her. "Get in," he ordered with an impatient sigh when she grimaced unwillingly at the rocks beneath her feet.

"No, thank you," she hissed.

"I said get in," Choya Barnett repeated crisply. "You might as well. A few yards down the road you'll probably end up with a twisted ankle or cut foot and you'll have to accept the offer anyway. Get in now and save yourself some pain. Besides, I'm going in your direction."

His logic made her pause. "You don't even know where I'm going," she accused.

"There's only one destination you could possibly have," he replied with thinning patience.

"Oh?" Her hands slipped challengingly to her hips. "And what is that?"

"The cemetery. Every tourist goes there." He sounded so insufferably certain that Jacquie was loath to admit he was right. The problem was, looking down the road toward her destination, there seemed to be nothing else she could be going to but that. "You don't expect me to think you're merely walking for exercise, do you?" Choya mocked.

"Just because you made a calculated guess," Jacquie muttered, "you don't have to be so smug just because you were right!"

"Then stop arguing and get in." Any disguise of impatience was dropped at the clipped order.

If it hadn't been for the rocks biting through her soles, she would have refused. Quite truthfully, she wanted the ride even if she questioned his motives for offering it.

"Where's Robbie?" she asked coldly as she minced her way across the rocks to slide into the passenger seat of the open jeep. "Did you leave him home today in case I might corrupt him by flirting with him some more?"

Tawny gold eyes bored into her for an instant before the jeep surged forward onto the highway. "Actually he happens to be in Sunday school."

Jacquie stared straight ahead. "It's a pity you didn't choose to avail yourself of some Christian teachings."

Her tongue was barbed, but her basic opinion of the man hadn't changed. He was coolly aloof and faintly condemning in his attitude, but he still attracted her. The chiseled features were unconventionally handsome in their ruthless strength and ruggedness.

With a flash of insight, Jacquie knew the key to his attraction. Choya Barnett was flagrantly male, more virile and masculine than anyone she had ever personally come in contact with before. His physique unconsciously boasted of it, from long, muscular legs, narrowed waist and hips tapering out to solid chest and wide shoulders and ending with dark looks. It was his eyes, the tawny gold of a mountain cat, that heightened the primitive look. They were a gold mask of cynical aloofness, spellbinding and unrevealing.

"I had other things I had to do," Choya stated.

Jacquie looked at him blankly, so lost in her contemplation of him that she had forgotten her previous comment. When his gaze swung to her, she felt the force of his male vitality.

"What?" She swallowed back the sensation of being jolted to her toes.

"I said," he repeated dryly, "that I had other things I had to do besides going to church."

The indifference in his look cut her. It was easy to return a caustic reply when his brief glance swept over her and back to the road.

"Very important things like keeping track of my whereabouts." The cool toss of her head was at odds with the green blue glitter of battle in her eyes.

The jeep slowed and bounced into the graveled parking lot, stopping in front of the butting stick fence protecting the cemetery. Weathered markers were visible beyond the closed fence. Against the skyline were rising mountains, barren and grim. At their feet were the undulating plains of sand and sage and cactus.

Without a thank-you or goodbye, Jacquie slid out of the passenger seat, wincing as her thin soles felt the sharp gravel again. There was a fine film of dust on her white slacks. She slapped it off, wishing perversely it was Choya's face she was hitting instead of her legs. Refusing to look at the jeep, she stalked toward the gift shop that housed the entrance to the cemetery.

"One of the things I wanted to do," Choya's low voice came from directly behind her, stopping her short, "was talk to you."

Pivoting sharply, Jacquie tilted her head challengingly to one side. "I can't think of a thing you could possibly want to discuss with me. I know you don't intend to apologize for your rudeness yesterday." But there was a questioning lift to her voice on the last statement.

"No, I'm not going to apologize," he answered smoothly.

Her lips tightened and she spun toward the door. "Then we can't have anything to talk about."

If he had apologized, she discovered, she had the eerie feeling she would have completely succumbed to his dangerous attraction.

The gift-shop door she yanked open wouldn't slam shut. It was held by his strong hand. She might not want to hear what Choya Barnett wanted to say to her, but he was definitely following her with the intention that she should.

In the shop, she stopped, searching impatiently for the exit door to the cemetery. A strong hand impersonally took hold of her elbow and guided her to the right.

"This way," he told her.

Aware of the curious and interested looks from the clerk and other tourists as they made their way to the exit door, Jacquie tried to ease the look of displeasure from her face. Outdoors, they had traveled several paces before his hand fell away.

Taking deep, calming breaths, Jacquie resolved to remain as composed and controlled as he was—and as indifferent to his presence as he was to hers. At a strolling pace, she started wandering among the tombstone markers, the wind-and-sand-smoothed rocks making an uneven path for her feet. Sage and cactus and twisting, gnarled bushes grew rampant in the graveyard, nearly obscuring some markers.

The emptiness of the surrounding country-side stretched away from the rocky hill where the remains of the Western frontiersmen lay. The land appeared barren and virtually un-marked by the passage of time and civiliza-tion. The ghosts of Apache warriors walked the distant mountains that rose into the blue sky.

Shielding her eyes with a hand against the climbing angle of the morning sun, Jacquie studied the mountain-crested horizon. Choya Barnett was standing behind her and slightly to her right. An inner radar seemed to pinpoint his location when her peripheral vision failed to see him.

"The Dragoon Mountains," he informed her, obviously following the direction of her gaze.

"That's where your ranch is, isn't it?" Her gaze ran the length of the mountains, her in-terest increased in spite of a silent effort to deny it.

"Robbie told you?"

"Yes." Jacquie glanced over her shoulder to bring the impassive face into her vision. His measured look was difficult to hold. She turned the rest of the way around, pretending an interest in a plain wooden cross at the head of a rocky grave. "As a matter of fact he did tell me."

"It's Robbie I wanted to talk to you about."

"Oh?" Aquamarine eyes darted coolly to the gold mask of his watchful gaze. "What about Robbie?"

"He's going to be spending the day in town again. Tombstone is too small for the two of you not to meet sometime."

"And?" Jacquie prodded, finding a seething anger beginning to build.

"And I would prefer that you don't encourage him to become more friendly," he stated.

"What am I supposed to do?" she challenged him icily. "Tell him to get lost?"

"I'm certain someone like you can push him casually away without resorting to deliberate cruelty." There was a faintly contemptuous curl of his upper lip.

"Someone like me?" Jacquie arched an eyebrow in his direction. "What's that supposed to mean?"

"Miss Grey, that combination of corn silk hair, turquoise eyes and a curving figure is sure to have brought you a string of admirers, some wanted and some not." Cynical mockery edged his low voice. "You undoubtedly have had a great deal of experience in tactfully telling an unwanted admirer to get lost. A little boy should be easy to handle."

"Why should I?" she shrugged, moving nonchalantly on to the next rock-mounded grave. "I mean other than the fact you obviously don't like me."

His jaw tightened. "My son has the painful habit of forming passionately intense attachments to people, especially strangers. He expects them to feel the same. When they leave, as you will some time tomorrow, he finds it impossible to understand why he's been rejected."

"I don't think I believe you, Mr. Barnett," Jacquie declared boldly. "At least, not totally. Robbie doesn't strike me as the type of child to go running around falling in love with strangers indiscriminately."

"He discriminates," Choya answered tautly, a vague cryptic note in his words.

For a moment she could only look at him curiously, trying to fathom the strange reply. Then the reason dawned on her. She should have guessed it before, but he had caught her off guard.

"Robbie only chooses blond-haired girls," Jacquie said softly, waiting for a sign to flicker across the strong face to indicate that she had guessed correctly. She couldn't be certain, but she thought his expression hardened. "Do I resemble his mother very much?" Her eyes gleamed brightly as they unflinchingly held the piercing alertness of his.

Surprisingly Choya was the first to look away. His slashing male profile was sharply defined by the blueness of the sky. Yet he didn't seem disturbed or disconcerted by her guess.

"Robbie obviously told you about Rosemary, too," he said thinly.

"He didn't mention his mother's name." An intense curiosity swept over Jacquie, surging through her veins with an overwhelming desire to find out how much she looked like Choya Barnett's late wife. "Am I very much like her?" she repeated.

Again the full brunt of his topaz-bright gaze was focused on her, skimming her features in quick assessment. Jacquie discovered she was holding her breath. A protest welled inside that she could look like anyone but herself.

"No," he denied in a quiet but emphatic voice. His attention shifted to a strand of pale, golden hair, which had fallen forward across her breast, and which contrasted with the lightweight blouse that was the same brilliant turquoise color as her eyes. "Your hair is the same shade of moonbeams trapped in a mountain pool," he murmured almost absently. His gaze was hard when it slashed back to her face. "But the comparison ends there. My wife had brown eyes and freckles sprinkled across her nose. She was small and delicately built, but every inch a tomboy. None of those descriptions would fit you."

"I quite agree," Jacquie answered, taking a deep breath and turning away. She had always been quite proud of her medium height and her slender, if definitely curvaceous, figure. He made them sound like a handicap. While she liked the outdoors, she found inside activities just as enjoyable.

"Unfortunately Robbie was too young when Rosemary was killed for him to have any memories of her. To him she's a beautiful blond woman in a photograph," Choya Barnett added in the same controlled even tone.

"Killed? How?" The question was out before Jacquie considered the wisdom of probing deeper into his personal life.

"A car accident—not that it really concerns you."

There was a slight shake of her head in apology. "I'm sorry."

"For prying, or that my wife is dead?"

Jacquie tensed. He was baiting her, trying to put her in her place. He would find she wasn't as malleable as he would like.

"For neither," she tilted her chin defiantly. "I wasn't conscious of prying, and only in an abstract way could I truthfully be sorry your wife died."

Choya smiled without humor. "Then why apologize?"

She didn't actually know why she had apologized. It had been an instinctive reaction. To admit that would only prompt further mockery from him. She had to bluff her way through.

"If I'm sorry about anything," Jacquie said slowly, considering her words as she issued them, "then it's the fact that Robbie is trying to transfer his need for a mother's love to me. I can't be blamed for that and I don't think it's fair that you should."

"I don't blame you." Choya stood before her, his bland expression unchanging as if carved in granite. "I'm merely asking you not to encourage him."

"Haven't you become tired of running around warning any strange blonde to stay away from your son?'' She forced a smile of amusement to her lips. "What Robbie is really seeking is the gentleness of a woman. With only you and his grandfather for family, he's surrounded by men. The solution is simple—I would have thought you would have solved it by now. Why don't you get married again, Mr. Barnett? Then you wouldn't be placing me or you in this awkward position."

A hard sound almost like laughter came from his throat. "Are you advocating that I marry someone simply to provide female companionship for my son?" Jacquie had no intention of falling into the trap he had set. Her eyes danced with subdued mischief.

"I'm sure you would derive some compensation out of the arrangement as well as Robbie."

"You make marriage sound very cold and calculating. Is that the way you see it?" Choya countered with a watchful narrowing of his gaze.

"No." In her mind, Jacquie pictured the marriage of her parents, an unusual combination of endearing friendship, combustible personalities and ready laughter. "That isn't my idea of marriage at all, but I thought it might be yours."

"Did you now?" A thumb hooked itself through a belt loop in an aloofly challenging manner. "And what is your idea of marriage?"

There was a complacent shimmer in her aquamarine eyes. "That, Mr. Barnett, is between me and the man I marry, whenever he comes along."

The hard line of his mouth curved into a cold, sardonic smile. "What is your policy in the meantime, Miss Grey? To love them all?" The gold fire of his gaze burned over the jutting roundness of her breasts. "You can't land every man who walks by."

Again Jacquie felt a surge of antagonism. It was on the tip of her tongue to inform him that going braless was the fashion, but she checked the impulse. Using her long fingernails, she raked the silken silver screen of her hair away from her face and cast him a deliberately provocative glance.

"No, but you can try," she murmured, and turned away, but not before she noticed the flash of disgust.

Inwardly she shrugged that it didn't matter. From the moment they had met, Choya Barnett had condemned her as a tramp, so it would be useless to try to convince him otherwise. Besides, there was little excitement in this isolated town, so she might as well make some of her own. She'd be leaving in the morning.

With an exaggerated sway of her hips, she picked her way along the wind-and-sand-eroded rocks that formed the path at the foot of the graves. There was a scattering of Chinese names on the headstones. Others were marked with a name and a date and the starkly simple epitaph—Killed by Indians. Only one drew a shudder from Jacquie. It was the grave of a man who had known the swift and not always sure justice of the frontier West and was Hanged by Mistake.

At the tombstones of the Clantons and the McLaurys, Jacquie read the inscription with surprise, then instinctively she turned to the man who silently followed her.

She asked him for an explanation.

"It says they were murdered. Weren't they killed in a gunfight at the OK Corral?" she questioned.

"Yes." A sun-browned hand cupped a match flame to his cigarette, protecting the fire from the teasing breeze. "But the Clantons were very popular in Tombstone. The same can't be said for Wyatt Earp and his brothers. For a while there was considerable question whether it was a fair fight."

"Was it?" Jacquie tipped her head to the side curiously.

"It depends on whether you were talking to one of the Clantons's friends or an Earp supporter." Choya exhaled a cloud of smoke, pinching the match between his fingers. "The general consensus now seems to be that it was."

As she digested the information, Jacquie moved toward the entrance to the gift shop. The long, cylindrical stalks of a cactus plant caught her attention and she paused beside it. Its wayward growth resembled a pincushion, minus the cushion.

"What kind of a cactus is this?" Her lashes veiled the dancing gleam in her eyes.

"An ocotillo," Choya answered, pronouncing the double *l* sound as a *y*. The faint narrowing of his eyes revealed that he had guessed she had been wondering if it was the cactus of his namesake. "The fence separating the parking lot from the cemetery is made from the stalks of the ocotillo. It was a common practice years ago to make solid stick corrals from the ocotillo because of the absence of lumber in this desert region."

"It doesn't look very substantial," Jacquie mused, studying the parking-lot fence.

"The thorns are just about as effective as barbed wire."

"I suppose so," she agreed, and walked on.

"You still haven't given me your answer, Miss Grey." He reached around her and opened the door to the gift shop.

For an instant, the carved male features were close to her own face and Jacquie's heart turned over. A searing fire flashed through her veins. The impulse again returned with instinctive swiftness to feel the hard pressure of his mouth against her own.

This time she didn't give in to the desire as she had done the last time. The totally elemental reaction she had to him whenever he was near unnerved her.

"What answer?" The blankness was not deliberate. Jacquie was gaining time for her senses to recover so she could think clearly.

The clerk in the gift shop glanced up when they entered. Choya smiled thinly and nodded, a flicker of impatience in his tawny gaze. There was no one else in the shop and Jacquie guessed by his silence that he didn't want the clerk overhearing their conversation.

His hand firmly grasped her elbow and escorted her out the door to the parking lot, releasing her immediately. Her skin tingled where his fingers had made their imprint.

"I asked that you wouldn't encourage my son, and I want your answer that you won't," Choya demanded calmly as they paused beside the jeep.

Her tongue ran thoughtfully over the whiteness of her teeth. The indifferent set of his expression prodded her into a boldness that bordered on rashness. She was not accustomed to being spurned.

"What would you do if I don't give you the answer you want?" she challenged with a sweep of her lashes.

There was a faint distension in his nostrils, but no other outward display of emotion. "What is your answer?" Choya Barnett refused to acknowledge her question.

The temptation was there to let him wonder, to ignore his question as he had ignored hers. It would anger him, she knew. If he became angry enough, he might ... With an impatient toss of her silvery blond hair, she looked away from the pinning fascination of his tawny gold gaze, dangerously compelling.

"If I see Robbie, I'll be polite and friendly," she declared. Her turquoise green eyes snapped back to his face, irritated that she was so attracted to the man as to desire his anger rather than his indifference. "But I assure you I will make it clear that I'm leaving tomorrow—so clear that it will be just short of the point of bluntness. Does that satisfy you?''

There was a glitter of lazy satisfaction in his eyes. ''Yes, it does. Would you like a lift back to your motel?''

Jacquie pursed her lips together, wishing to deny his offer, but the painful memory of the sharp gravel on the roadside insisted that logically she must accept.

''If I wouldn't be taking you out of your way,'' she agreed with a saccharine smile.

Now that Choya Barnett had received the answer he wanted, he didn't appear to think it was necessary to maintain a conversation. The ride was short and Jacquie kept her attention diverted from the man behind the wheel. But she couldn't ignore the virility emanating from the muscularly firm body of the driver. Only when he had let her out in front of her motel room did she allow her eyes to watch him, and then it was from the window of her room.

For nearly two hours, she alternately paced the confines of the small room and lounged on the bed. Her restlessness increased with each ticking second until she felt she would scream if she stayed in the room another minute.

The subconscious decision not to appear in town at all was cast aside. So it would displease Choya Barnett if she ran into his son in town—so what? She had not promised that she wouldn't see Robbie, only that she wouldn't encourage his friendship. There was no need to voluntarily condemn herself into making a prison out of her motel room.

Sliding her rose-shaded sunglasses onto her nose, she picked up her oversized leather bag and walked out, locking the door behind her. With a map from the motel room pointing out the buildings of historical significance, she wandered along the old streets, pausing in front of some buildings and entering others that were open.

Once she saw Robbie aimlessly hobbling along the board sidewalk and she darted into a building before he saw her. Truthfully she would have welcomed the company of the small boy—perhaps because she recognized the wild, impetuous streak within Robbie that had prompted him to ride a bull calf. It was a trait she shared with him, that and the occasional loneliness of being an only child.

Late in the afternoon the rumblings of her stomach reminded Jacquie that she hadn't eaten since breakfast. The painted sign of a restaurant beckoned her down Allen Street, and she was nearly at the door when she heard the thumping of a pair of crutches behind her.

"Jacquie!" Robbie's voice called her name eagerly. "Wait!"

Biting her lip, she started to ignore him, then realized it was useless. He was too close. Fixing a bland smile on her face, she stopped and pivoted around.

"Hello, Robbie," she greeted him politely, but taking care not to sound too warm. "How are you today?"

"Fine. I was beginning to think I wouldn't see you today. Where have you been?"

"In my motel room mostly," Jacquie lied.

"What were you doing there?" Pale brown eyes rounded curiously.

"Resting. I have a long drive ahead of me tomorrow," keeping to her promise that she would make it clear to the boy that she was leaving.

The corners of his mouth drooped. "Do you have to go?"

"Of course," Jacquie laughed, instilling deliberately careless unconcern in the sound despite the twinge of guilt at the dullness that clouded his face. "I wouldn't have been here at all if it wasn't for the damage to my car. I have to go to Los Angeles."

"Why?"

It was a good question. Jacquie simply shrugged indifferently. "Because I do, that's all.'' The subject needed changing. "Where's your father?"

"At a meeting." Robbie leaned heavily on his crutches. "He'll be coming pretty soon, I suppose."

"Well, you'd better wait here for him," she said with false brightness, and started to turn away.

"Where are you going?" The wooden crutches were quickly shifted to follow her.

"Into the restaurant to have something to eat." Her hunger was growing with each minute. She didn't intend to deny herself food just to avoid Robbie.

"Can I come with you?" he asked eagerly.

"I don't think that's a good idea," Jacquie inserted quickly. "How will your father know where you are?"

"He'll find me," Robbie replied with certainty. Then there was a flash of hesitancy. Brown eyebrows straightened into a line. "Am I bothering you? Dad says I bother people and that they really don't want me around."

Jacquie could see that Robbie was mentally bracing himself for a rejection. He had suddenly seen through her subtle attempts to be rid of him and was experiencing the searing and painful truth. Damn Choya Barnett, she raged silently. What harm could it possibly do to spend a few minutes with the boy?

"Heavens, no, you don't bother me!" She flashed him a brilliant smile. "I like you, Robbie. I just didn't want you to get into any trouble with your dad by coming into the restaurant with me. If you don't think he'll mind, why don't you come in with me and have a milk shake while I eat?" Silently, Jacquie added that his father could get just as angry as he liked because she had broken her promise.

"A banana milk shake!" Robbie declared with a wide grin of acceptance.

CHAPTER FOUR

ROBBIE SLURPED noisily on his straw, sucking up the last drop of milk shake from his glass. Jacquie smiled inwardly at the sound and sipped at her iced tea. The bell above the restaurant door jingled, signaling the entrance of a customer.

The straw remained in Robbie's mouth, his hands around the glass, as he glanced over the rim at the door. Spiky lashes quickly veiled the pale brown of his eyes.

Jacquie tensed, her chin jerking slightly upward an instant before the footsteps stopped at their table. There was a blaze of gold over her features, the eyes of a mountain cat that had found its prey.

"Well, hello, Mr. Barnett." She cast him a dazzling smile of feigned surprise.

"Miss Grey," Choya Barnett returned the greeting tautly.

"Hello, Dad," Robbie added brightly. "I was just keeping Jacquie company while she ate her dinner."

"So I see." He remained standing, towering above them both as if contemplating which of them to pounce on first. Robbie squirmed uncomfortably and it took all of Jacquie's willpower not to do the same. Choya picked up the crutches leaning against a chair and pointedly handed them to Robbie. "You can go out to the jeep. I'll only be a few minutes."

"Yes sir." Robbie didn't even glance at Jacquie as he balanced himself on the crutches and proceeded from the restaurant.

Resentment flashed with fiery blue green flames in her eyes, but she concealed it by making a show of searching through her bag for her wallet. With the wallet and the check for the meal in her hand, she rose from the table, brushing past Choya as if he wasn't even there.

"Do you always break your promises so casually, Miss Grey?" he accused in a low voice.

"Yes!" she hissed, waiting impatiently at the cash register while the waitress rang up the amount and gave her the correct change. When they stepped outside, Jacquie finished speaking the heated words burning the tip of her tongue. "Especially I break them when a little boy asks if he's bothering me because he's lonely. And for your information, I met him only as I was going into the restaurant. I haven't been with him all afternoon."

"Sometimes it's kinder to be cruel. I thought I explained that," Choya retorted.

"It's easy for you to say that." She was breathing heavily now, with anger. "Being cruel probably comes naturally to you!"

His hand snaked out to seize her wrist, yanking her toward him. Jacquie was a hair's breadth away from discovering how accurate her statement was. But his action knocked the large bag from her hand. She hadn't bothered to fasten the clasp and its contents spilled over the boardwalk and into the street.

"Look what you've done!" she snapped, and wrenched her wrist free of his hold, uncaring that the accident had granted her a reprieve from his anger.

As she stooped to begin gathering the scattered contents, Robbie came hobbling from the jeep parked in front of the restaurant. "I'll help, Jacquie," he offered.

He maneuvered himself into a sitting position on the board sidewalk and began picking up the items that had rolled into the street. Picking up a tube of lipstick near the pointed toe of Choya Barnett's boot, Jacquie glared up.

"You could help," she accused.

Then she wished she had said nothing as he bent down beside her, dark umber brown hair waving thickly beneath the band of his Stetson hat. Unceremoniously he began dumping items back in her handbag with no regard for neatness or order. With her heartbeat quickening at the sight of the rippling muscles beneath his shirt, Jacquie soon didn't care either, anxious only to be out of range of his animal attraction.

When all the items Robbie had gathered were back in her bag, Jacquie moved swiftly to the edge of the sidewalk, holding the large bag open for his handful. This time she closed it securely and stayed well away from Choya's reach.

"Would you like a ride back to your motel?" Robbie asked.

Smiling tightly, Jacquie shook her head, refusing to even glance at his father. "No, thank you. I'm not going back right now."

The real truth was she didn't want to ride with Choya. At this hour, there were very few places she could go, except to a saloon. She might have a wild streak, but it wasn't so strong that she would venture into a strange bar alone. She would walk slowly back to the motel, but she wouldn't accept the offer of a ride.

"Goodbye, Robbie." She bent down and offered her hand to the boy. "You take care of yourself."

He shook it solemnly, a glimmer of apprehension in his pale brown eyes, but no tears. "Goodbye, Jacquie."

She straightened, meeting the impenetrable mask of his father. "Goodbye, Mr. Barnett." She didn't offer him her hand, letting her fingers curl around the strap of the handbag. "It's been an experience running into you."

His alert gaze ran over the taunting smile on her face, his mouth quirking at one corner. But he didn't respond to her play on words. "Goodbye, Miss Grey," in a very final tone.

As Choya moved to help Robbie into the jeep, Jacquie turned away and began walking down the street in the opposite direction of her motel. She pretended an interest in the contents of a shop window until she heard the jeep start and pull away from the curb. She glanced over her shoulder and waved once more to Robbie.

When they were out of sight, she felt crazily alone. The sun was touching the roofs on its downward slide. Sighing unconsciously, she turned and started walking toward her motel. Tomorrow she would be gone, and all that had happened to her here would become a humorous story she would relate at some party or other. In a way, it hardly seemed right.

That night Jacquie slept soundly, not waking until well after eight in the morning. She showered quickly and packed the suitcase she had brought to the motel, setting it beside the door so she could pick it up when she came back with her car.

With the strap of her bag slung over one shoulder, she tucked one side of her unnaturally thick blond hair behind an ear and started for the garage. Snug-fitting jeans in a faded blue molded the long length of her legs. The navy blue knit top with its stitched-on star in the center left little to the imagination.

In the short walk to the garage, two cars stopped to offer her a lift, but Jacquie waved them on. Hitchhiking was not her idea of safe travel. As she was crossing the highway to the garage, she saw the mechanic standing beside the gas pumps.

"Hi! Is my car fixed?" she called to him.

He nodded and waited until she was closer to answer. "It's all ready for you, just like a brand new one."

"I hope it doesn't cost like a new one," Jacquie laughed as she followed him into the small office. "I couldn't afford it."

The man laughed briefly in return and picked up an itemized bill from a cluttered desk top. "I tried to be as fair as I could," he replied, handing it to her.

The curved brim of the man's cap was pulled low over his receding hairline, hiding his eyes. Yet Jacquie could feel the slow appraisal of his gaze moving over her while she studied the bill. She was too accustomed to such looks to be insulted. There was no harm in looking or thinking. And she knew how to handle those who weren't satisfied with that.

"It all seems to be in order." She breathed in deeply, glancing from the paper to give the mechanic a dazzling smile. The total wasn't as much as his estimate had been.

"I overestimated the labor cost a bit," the mechanic explained, his eyes brightening at her smile. "I never worked on that model of a car before and I wasn't sure how long it would take."

"I appreciate your honesty."

Sliding the strap from her shoulder, she set her bag on a fairly empty corner of the desk and unfastened the clasp. She hadn't bothered to put the contents in order after they had spilled in the street the afternoon before. She began sifting through the oversized bag, searching for her wallet.

"That's the trouble with big bags," she smiled ruefully. "They hold so much that you never can find anything when you want it."

There was an understanding gleam in the man's eyes that said he could patiently wait all day. A twinge of fear raced through her when her rummaging search didn't produce the wallet. Smiling nervously, she began taking the larger items out and placing them on the desk beside her bag. Soon the bottom of the bag was in sight and still no wallet.

"It can't be gone!" she breathed with a touch of panic, and began going through the articles she had laid on the desk. The wallet wasn't among them. Raking her fingernails through the waving thickness of her white gold hair, she paused in her search, troubled turquoise green eyes meeting the questioning glance of the mechanic. "My wallet's gone. It has all my money and my credit cards and my identification—everything."

"Are you sure you didn't leave it somewhere?" he suggested.

"No, I didn't." She shook her head, then hesitated. "At least—may I use your telephone?"

"Of course." He turned the black phone on his desk toward her. "Be my guest."

Hurriedly Jacquie telephoned the restaurant where she had eaten the previous afternoon and asked if her wallet had been turned in. At the negative answer, she explained that she had spilled the contents of her handbag outside the door and asked if someone would check to see if it had rolled under the board sidewalk.

After waiting for heart-pounding seconds while it was checked, the answer was still no. A phone call to the police department met with the same answer that it hadn't been turned in. Whoever had found it had obviously kept it or thrown it away where no one else would find it.

When she hung up the telephone, her mind was frantically searching for a solution. What was she going to do without money?

"Maybe you could have left it in the motel?" The mechanic studied the white teeth thoughtfully nibbling at her lower lip, his expression concerned, yet reserved.

"No," Jacquie sighed. "I packed everything before I came here. If it was there, I would have found it."

"I wish there was something I could do," the man murmured sympathetically.

"Maybe," hope glimmered, "you could." It was one thing to be flat broke and another to be broke and on foot. "I need my car."

"Well..." the mechanic faltered, glancing at the itemized bill lying on his desk.

"I'd pay you back, I promise," Jacquie rushed, "just as soon as I found a job. Every dime of it."

The man readjusted the cap on his head, plainly reluctant to agree. Jacquie's father had often accused her of depending more on her feminine allure than her intelligence. It had often proved the easiest means of getting her way. "Honestly!" Her brilliantly expressive eyes darted to the name stitched above the pocket of his overalls.

"Bob, I need my car, and you can trust me to pay the bill."

"Miss Grey, I..." He shifted uncomfortably, his mouth curving weakly to return the faintly coaxing smile of her glistening lips. "I don't really see how I could. This is just a small garage and your bill is a lot of money for me to carry."

"I know," she agreed, moving toward him and letting her hand rest on his forearm. "But I really need my car," she pleaded earnestly. Her fingers dug slightly into the muscle of his arm in a desperately clutching manner as if he was the only one in the world she could turn to for help.

He swallowed nervously, his gaze focused on her moist, parted lips. She could sense that he was weakening and felt a rush of power. Some men were so easily maneuvered.

"I'd do anything," she added the breathy promise with suggestive emphasis on the last word.

A redness began creeping up from the neckline of his shirt. His gaze fell away, hesitating for a tantalizing second on the rounded swell of her breasts, then focused on the desk top. Nervously he cleared his throat and Jacquie knew victory was within her grasp.

Until a low voice pulled it out of reach. "That's an all-inclusive statement. What's the problem, Miss Grey?"

At the sound of Choya Barnett's voice, Jacquie's lashes closed, but she didn't turn around. The mechanic took a quick, embarrassed step away from her, a dull red spreading across his cheeks.

"Well, Choya," the man said with a nervous tremor, "I didn't expect to see you in town today."

"I had to take Robbie to the doctor, then on to school," he explained, but Jacquie could tell that his piercing gaze had not left her back. "What seems to be the difficulty here?"

"Miss Grey," the mechanic darted her an anxious look, "lost her wallet or had it stolen. She, uh, doesn't have any money."

"You had the wallet yesterday at the restaurant," Choya stated flatly.

Jacquie breathed in deeply. How did he manage to always find her in the worst possible situation? With a defiant toss of her head, she glanced over her shoulder, her glittering jewel-colored eyes meeting the faint contempt in the metallic hardness of his gaze. The gold loop of her earring rested coolly along the side of her neck.

"Yes, I had it at the restaurant," she agreed with forced calm. "But if you remember, the contents of my handbag were accidently spilled as I was leaving. More than likely, my wallet wasn't put back in my bag and someone came along, found it, and didn't return it."

"Have you telephoned to be certain?" The skepticism in his tone rankled.

"I phoned the restaurant and the police," Jacquie replied shortly.

"Did you leave it at your motel?" His implication was obvious. He believed she had conveniently forgotten her wallet in the hope that she could trick her way out of paying the repair bill for her car.

"I did not."

"Perhaps we'd better go and check," Choya suggested with an arrogant and challenging flick of a dark eyebrow.

"By all means let's check." With a seething fury, Jacquie began stuffing the contents of her bag back into the bag.

How dared he accuse her of lying? Her smile to the mechanic was determinedly sweet. There was some measure of satisfaction in seeing Choya's mouth thin grimly in disgust at the smile. If she was going to be hanged as a tramp, she might as well act like one! After all, she thought sarcastically as she swept out through the door ahead of him, she didn't want to disappoint the autocratic Choya Barnett.

"My wallet won't be at the motel," she declared, sliding into the passenger seat of the jeep.

"Why? Did you hide it somewhere along the road on the way here?" he taunted harshly.

"No, I didn't!" Her temper flared. "It is truly missing."

There wasn't even a flicker of doubt in the tawny cat eyes. He didn't believe her. Trembling with anger, Jacquie folded her arms around her bulky handbag and stared straight ahead. Tears scaled her eyes, a result of the ferocity of her emotion.

With the engine growling steadily, Choya turned the jeep on to the main highway. "Save the tears," he jeered. "I don't buy the helpless female act."

"I always cry when I lose my temper!" Jacquie retorted in a choked voice. "I wouldn't waste tears trying to appeal to you."

"As long as we understand one another," he said indifferently.

"I understand you very well. You're as stubborn as a mule once you make up your mind about something or someone," she accused angrily. "I hope I'm around the day you also find out that you've made an ass of yourself."

"There is a possibility that your wallet is lost," he conceded dryly, "but nothing I've seen or heard would lead me to change my opinion of you."

A thousand insulting retorts sprang to mind, but Jacquie doubted that any of them would penetrate his thorny exterior. A cactus by name and a cactus by nature! She would be a fool to keep getting herself pricked. One of these times a thorn might find a more vulnerable spot than previous barbs had.

Keeping her mouth shut, she tossed him the key to her motel door when he stopped the jeep. She took a firm hold on her temper and blinked away the few hot tears before following him to the door. With her gaze focused on a point between the wide shoulders, it was difficult not to remember the last time he had been in her room and the searing briefness of his kiss.

His aggressively masculine presence dominated the small room. The unmade bed suddenly seemed to suggest an intimacy that disturbed Jacquie's senses. She paused inside the doorway and leaned against the wall, folding her arms in front of her.

"Search away, Mr. Barnett," she invited. "I would help, but I wouldn't want you to accuse me later on of hiding the wallet somewhere."

His gaze flicked sharply to her, then scanned the room. She watched his methodical search. The motel room was sparsely furnished and it took little time before he had completed.

"Perhaps you should go through my luggage," Jacquie suggested caustically. "I might have secreted it somewhere among my clothes."

Choya glanced at the suitcase near her feet. "I accept that your wallet is missing and, I presume, all your money with it."

"Every cent of it, except three pennies that were loose in the bottom of my handbag. Plus my credit cards and my identification, not to mention pictures and a lot of other things that can't be replaced." Her chin was thrust forward at a rebellious angle. "I'm completely destitute, with the exception of my clothes and my car, which is in the garage with a large repair bill owing on it."

"The accident was your fault." He stood in the center of the room, tall and decidedly in command. "You can't blame me for the damage to your car."

"I don't." She released an angry breath and straightened away from the wall.

"Do you have any family or friends that you might call?"

"Yes." But she would almost rather starve to death than call home, running to her parents for help when she had only been on her own for less than a week.

"I suggest you call them," Choya said briskly, his tone bordering on an order.

Jacquie slid a hand through her hair, shaking its length down her back. As much as she resented his suggestion and dreaded making the phone call, it was the only logical solution now. Without money, how could she find a place to sleep or buy food or anything?

Sighing, she walked to the telephone beside the bed and placed a collect call to her home. She crossed her fingers, feeling stupidly superstitious, and offered a silent prayer that her mother would answer the telephone.

"A collect call from whom?" Her father's voice boomed at the other end of the line.

"Dad, it's me, Jacquie," she rushed, but the operator broke in, asking again if he would accept the reversed charges.

"No, I won't, by God!" he declared. "She wanted to be on her own, and if she wants to talk to me bad enough, she'll pay for the phone call herself." And the receiver was slammed down.

Jacquie thanked the operator and replaced the telephone. Her teeth sank into her lower lip. Considering how vehement she had been in declaring her independence, she could hardly blame her father. Proudly she lifted her head and met Choya's speculating gaze.

"They wouldn't accept the call," she informed him, adopting an air of unconcern. The truth was it hurt, probably as much as she had hurt her parents.

"There's no one else you can call?"

Jacquie considered her girlfriend Tammy in Bisbee, but as Tammy was newly married, she knew that her friend's finances wouldn't stretch to the amount Jacquie needed.

She shook her head. "No. That's all right," she shrugged nonchalantly. "I'll get by."

"How?" he challenged.

"I'll find a way," she declared.

"Like today," Choya taunted, "when you were trying to trick Bob into letting you take your car without paying him for the repairs."

"I would have paid him!" Jacquie flashed.

"Yes," his mouth quirked sardonically. "I'd forgotten you vowed you would do *anything*." His dark head was tilted to one side, his carved features coldly cynical. "What would you have done if he had taken you at your word?"

"I could have handled him," she answered confidently. At the skeptical curl of his lip, she added, "I started filling out my jeans when I was twelve. I know something about men and how to make them think the way I want them to."

Amusement teased the corners of his mouth. "That sounds like a childish boast," he taunted, his gold look sweeping insolently over her.

Childish? A finely arched brow shot up. The glove of challenge had been thrown down and Jacquie was not the type to ignore it.

"Do you know what you sound like?" she murmured, wandering with seemingly aimless purpose toward him, her thumbs hooked in the waistband of her jeans. Her head was tipped back, rippling silver gold hair streaming down her back. "You sound as though you're sorry I didn't come to you for help. Do you want me to ask you for money?"

Something harsh flickered across his chiseled features, a suggestion of savagery that was quickly gone. Jacquie had seen it, but she kept the knowledge from being revealed in her eyes as she returned his speculating study.

"Would you make me the same promise of 'anything' as an incentive?" The hard mouth quirked cynically. "And forget to keep it?"

"I wouldn't forget." She moistened her lips, her gaze running provocatively over his wide shoulders, then to his masculinely compelling features. "In fact, keeping a promise like that might even be fun."

A muscle twitched along his powerful jawline. "Do you think so?"

"I know so," Jacquie replied with an almost kittenish purr. "Don't you?"

"No."

"You still don't trust me, do you?" she laughed throatily. "You still think that I might cheat you in some way. I wouldn't, though. I always pay my debts in full."

In a fluid movement, she eliminated the distance that separated them. Her hands spread over his chest to the width of his shoulders, then circled them while she pressed her soft curves against his granite length. His fingers gripped her hip bones, tightening as if to shove her away, then hesitated.

Jacquie smiled slowly, certain now that she hadn't made a mistake. She knew what was going on in his mind. Little did he know that he was playing right into her hands. Men, she thought smugly, if they only knew how easy they were to manipulate!

"Are you beginning to see how much fun it could be, Choya?" speaking his name with a seductively husky pitch to her voice.

She heard the hiss of his sharply indrawn breath. Her fingers slid into the umber brown thickness of the hair at the back of his neck. Raising on tiptoes, she touched her lips against the firm line of his mouth. Persuasively she began kissing him, lightly, tantalizing, until his mouth was not quite so stiff beneath hers.

The musky scent of shaving lotion clung to the sun-browned skin of his smooth cheeks, a heady combination with the warm, male scent of his body. Her heart quickened its beat, a pagan drumbeat to match her role as the temptress.

Pliantly she molded her body more firmly against him, letting him take her weight. The stamp of his virility was marked in every muscled inch of him, proof that he couldn't resist her feminine offering indefinitely.

Her kiss deepened with unforced passion, and his hard mouth answered the pressure, although the initiative remained hers. With a shuddering sigh, almost of regret, Jacquie disentangled her lips from his, sliding her hands from the muscled column of his neck to his shoulders.

Through the curling sweep of her lashes, she looked into the tawny gold of his eyes. They were still infuriatingly unrevealing, as was the impassive expression carved in the bold lines of his face.

"Now do you see?" she purred.

With the swiftness of a striking serpent, her hand lashed out at his cheek, a satisfying sting in her palm. Her eyes blazed with the fires of revenge as she twisted free of the large hands on her hips.

"But I would never come to you!" she hissed as his cold surprise turned to icy fury. "I would never ask you for money if you possessed all the wealth on earth! Your opinion of me is nothing compared to my opinion of you! You, with your superior airs and your smug arrogance! You think you know me, but you don't know me at all! I don't need your help. I don't need anybody's help!"

"Don't you?" Choya countered in a voice so low and so controlled that it was almost frightening.

Her lips parted slightly in surprise. She had expected retaliation—verbal abuse, a barrage of insults, but not this ominous silence. Her anger evaporated with chilling swiftness as he pivoted away.

Stunned, she watched him, unable to believe that she could assault his ego without receiving some repercussions. She had felt safe pretending to seduce him because she had known he didn't want her. He considered her disgusting and had only played along to see how far she would go. She had known all this, had guessed it, had planned her action around this knowledge.

But now—now, she didn't feel safe. His reaction had not followed the expected pattern. Choya wasn't even making an outraged exit. He was walking toward the unmade bed.

CHAPTER FIVE

HIS OBJECTIVE wasn't the bed. It was the telephone. Without a glance at Jacquie, he picked up the receiver and dialed a number. She was still staring at him in shock when he turned around to hold her gaze.

"Bob?" he said into the receiver. "This is Choya. How much was Miss Grey's repair bill...? Send it to me. I'll be by to pick up the car later today."

Her mouth opened to protest, but nothing came out. Her gaze followed the black receiver as it was returned to its cradle. Tremors of fear quaked through her, turning her bones to liquid jelly.

"You're expensive, Jacquie." His low-timbred voice said her name with insulting emphasis. "It's going to take some time to get my money's worth."

Her gaze flew to his face, the uncanny cat-like eyes glittering now at his trapped prey. His lips curled with sardonic amusement at her frightened look.

"You can't be serious," she breathed.

A dark eyebrow arched in arrogant mockery. "You put the proposition to me."

"I didn't proposition you!" Jacquie protested in shocked astonishment.

"What would you like to call it? Bribery?" Choya returned.

"I..." she faltered, the words stammering off the end of her flustered tongue, "I told you I...I would never c-come to you."

"Suit yourself." The wide shoulders shrugged with his even reply. "But it's the only way you'll get your car."

"You can't keep it. It's mine," she declared frantically.

"Possession is nine-tenths of the law." There was a wicked glint in his eyes. "The car is mine until the debt against it is paid in full. Either pay me the money or we'll revert to the old system of bartering goods and services for payment."

Jacquie swallowed. "I'll send you the money, I swear I will."

The harsh grooves on either side of his mouth deepened. "As you pointed out, I don't trust you. Payment in advance is the only thing I'll accept. Only when the full amount of the bill is satisfied will the car be yours again."

Appealing to him was useless. Jacquie reached down into her shaken depths for a bit of bravado. She slid the tips of her trembling hands into the pockets of her jeans and boldly met his look.

"All right, I'll pay you," she agreed. "I'll get a job and earn the money."

Her assertion only seemed to amuse him further. "Doing what, and where? Not here in Tombstone. The tourist season is over. There aren't any jobs to be had. What would you do for a place to sleep and food to eat in the meantime? I'm offering you both for the same price you'd have to pay to any other man."

"There are people other than men on this earth!" Jacquie fired back, his logic cornering her.

"But your feminine wiles wouldn't work very well on a woman," Choya reminded her. "What do you intend to do about your motel bill? The manager is a woman and I don't think she'd take it kindly if you tried to skip out without paying. In the eyes of the law, you're a vagrant with no visible means of support and no money and no possessions of any value."

"I have my car."

"No, I have your car." He smiled coldly. "You owe me for the repairs."

"You can't expect me to agree to let you—" Jacquie couldn't even get the words out. Her head drew back in negative denial. "You know how I feel about you. How unwilling I would be to have you—" Again the words lodged.

"Unwilling?" A humorless chuckle sounded deep in his throat. "You wouldn't be unwilling—not a girl like you."

"Stop it!" She was trembling now, her blood turning to ice. "You're simply trying to frighten me. You wouldn't dare touch me."

The tawny yellow eyes never left her face as he moved lazily toward her. Jacquie's first impulse was to retreat, but that was what he wanted her to do. He was planning to intimidate her until she cowered before him, humbly begging for his mercy. So Jacquie stood her ground, refusing to give him the satisfaction he sought and not believing for an instant that he meant to carry out his threat.

When he stopped in front of her, Choya reached out and caught a handful of hair. It shimmered white gold against his sun-browned fingers. Jacquie didn't move. She wouldn't struggle like a mouse under a cat's paw.

Through half-closed eyes, he studied her unyielding expression. Thick, dark brown lashes veiled the amber caution light that might have warned Jacquie she had underestimated him again. His fingers wound cruelly into her hair, roughly jerking her head farther back. The need to relieve the shooting pain in her scalp brought her voluntarily against him.

His free hand closed over the rounded fulness of her breast. Jacquie stiffened, pride saving her at the last minute from jerking away from the intimacy of his touch. She would not struggle like a frightened animal. He was only toying with her, she reminded herself.

But her heart was pounding against her ribs like a terrified bird beating its wings against the bars of a cage. His mouth had begun a slow descent toward hers, drawing out the seconds until she wanted to scream. Then the hard kiss was bruising her lips, crushing their softness against her teeth.

Her senses were clamoring to be recognized as she fought to ignore the salty taste of blood in her mouth. The pain in her scalp had stopped and the iron band of his arm had her in a vice grip. An ounce more of pressure and she was certain her spine would snap.

Searing flames had begun to lick through the lower half of her body where his muscled thighs had burned his brand into her skin. The suffocation of his kiss and his hold was draining her strength. The hands that she had held rigidly at her side were now raised to strain against the rippling muscles of his upper arms. She needed air to keep the whirling blackness from taking possession.

Choya allowed the one gasp for air as he freed her lips and began a rough exploration of the sensitive cord in her neck and the hollow of her throat. Involuntary shivers of sensual excitement tingled down her spine. Primitive instinct had her breasts swelling against the knit material of her top.

He must have felt or sensed the betraying response of her flesh, for his mouth returned to her lips with a demanding expertise that parted them with consummate ease. Suddenly his virility and her sexual attraction to him became more than Jacquie could resist. With a shuddering moan, she surrendered to the savage pleasure of his embrace.

With a sweeping motion, she was lifted off her feet and cradled effortlessly in his arms. Automatically her hands wrapped themselves around his neck as his hard male lips maintained their ownership of hers. Lost in a world of sensual abandonment, Jacquie felt as if she was floating on a cloud, seeing wondrous, unknown horizons.

Then, beneath her, was the firmness of a mattress and the white crispness of a bed sheet. And Choya's mouth, which had let her see unseen sights, left hers and didn't return. Her arms were still around his neck, her fingers locked.

The shadowy bronze veil of her lashes lifted to gaze into the masculine features so close to her own with a vague sense of awe. The glittering gold light of his eyes was licking over the tousled silver blond of her hair against the pillow, the bemused desire in the turquoise green brilliance of her eyes, and the invitation written on her moist, parted lips.

"Unwilling?" A taunting smile spread across the mouth that had seconds ago destroyed her resistance.

Reality came back with a rush. Scorching heat flamed through her face and neck. His hand slid familiarly along her thigh as he straightened away from the bed. To deny completely the devastation he had caused would not have been believed.

Sliding awkwardly from the bed, Jacquie struggled to find the smallest measure of poise. "I was only playing along to see how far you would go," she declared tightly, sarcasm trembling on the edge of her voice. "I'm surprised you stopped so soon."

"Anticipation is sweet, like dessert at the end of a meal," Choya responded evenly, watching her harried movements away from him. "There's plenty of time."

There was an empty feeling in the pit of her stomach that bespoke her unsatisfied state. Her flesh still yearned for the exquisite roughness of his caress.

"That's where you're wrong," Jacquie snapped, "because I have no intention of agreeing to your insulting proposition."

His gaze narrowed. "What's your alternative?"

"Oh, don't worry," she breathed in with savage anger. "I'll pay you for the repair bill on my car. I'll go to Tucson—I'll find a job there."

He studied her with lazy amusement. "If you step one foot outside of the town limits of Tombstone without me, I'll notify the authorities that you're deliberately leaving without paying your bills."

"Are you threatening me?" Jacquie lifted her head in open defiance.

"I'm promising you. Unlike you, I keep my word. You pay me one way or another, or else you don't leave town."

Her tactics weren't working, so she tried another. "You're supposedly a respected and upstanding member of the community. How are you going to explain me away?'' she challenged.

"My father is getting old, and it's becoming difficult for him to get around any more. It's common knowledge that I've been considering hiring a housekeeper. No one will be surprised by your presence in my home,'' Choya replied without any hesitation. "In fact, it's only a matter of time before your misfortune of losing your wallet will circulate. A lot of people will probably consider that I'm doing a good turn by hiring you."

A bitter laugh slipped out of her throat. "You don't honestly think people are going to believe that I'm only your housekeeper?"

"It doesn't matter to me what they think." The line of his mouth curved in sardonic amusement. "It certainly won't affect my reputation. If anything, people in general like a man to be a bit of a rogue."

"It doesn't matter what they think of me, does it?" Jacquie accused.

"They'll think you're a young girl who's taken a job as my housekeeper to earn some money. If they suspect more than that, they won't say anything,'' Choya countered.

Jacquie was all out of arguments. He had blocked her at every turn until the only way out of this miserable situation seemed to be his way. Silently panicking, she couldn't believe the mess that she had got herself into this time.

"I simply can't do it." She shook her head hopelessly.

"You don't have any choice," he returned with certainty. "It won't really be so bad and it definitely won't last forever."

Jacquie turned away, hugging her arms around her waist. She would think of something. Her mind raced wildly in search of an answer.

"What about Robbie?" she offered. "Remember, you didn't want him to become too attached to me. It's bound to happen if I'm in the same house with him."

"It might do the boy some good," Choya answered as if he, too, had considered that aspect of the situation. "He'll find out what you're really like and end this childish infatuation. I'm willing to take the risk where he's concerned."

She caught back the sob of desperation before it escaped her lips. Was there nothing she could say or do to make him change his mind? If only she could take back the words that she could handle any man! She had certainly never met a man like Choya Barnett before or she never would have uttered such a foolish remark.

"Wait here," he ordered. "I'll be back in a few minutes."

Since her mind was still juggling alternative solutions, his words didn't immediately register. Not until she heard the motel-room door open and close did she realize what he had said. Spinning toward the closed door, she stared at it.

Where was he going? What was he doing? Why had he left her? In a flash, she flew to the window and looked out. The jeep was still parked in front, but Choya wasn't near it. Wildly, she searched for a sign of him, then saw him walking toward the motel lobby.

He must have interpreted her silence as an agreement to his proposal and was going to settle the bill for her lodging. Her gaze swerved back to the jeep, a dangerous plan forming in her mind.

Impetuously, she gathered up her handbag and suitcase and glanced out of the window again. Choya was disappearing into the lobby. She darted out of the room, tossed her belongings in the back of the jeep and slid behind the wheel.

It was a more than even trade—her car for his jeep. She reached for the ignition key. It wasn't there. Frantically, she checked to see if he had left it under the floor mat. Nothing.

She flipped down the visor, but it wasn't there, either.

Nibbling at her lower lip, she wondered if it was possible to hot-wire a jeep and said a silent prayer that she would remember what one of her boyfriends had told her about the way it was done. She leaned to the side, ducking her head beneath the steering column. Her long hair nearly brushed the sandy floor.

"Grand theft—auto," Choya said with mocking reproof.

Jacquie sat up with a start, knocking the back of her head against the steering wheel. She glanced at him angrily as she rubbed the injured spot. He reached in his pocket and took out the keys.

"Move over," he ordered.

Mutinously Jacquie stayed where she was. His expression hardened, the line of his mouth thinning with his patience. Choya leaned down, scooped her into his arms, dodging her swinging hand as he shoveled her into the passenger seat. She would have dashed out the open side, but his hand clamped down on her wrist to keep her in the jeep.

"This is kidnapping!" she accused with a hiss.

Her hair swung forward as she whirled to face him, a rippling curtain of the palest spun gold. Strong fingers continued biting into the bone of her wrist, cutting off the circulation with bruising force.

Choya studied her coldly, an almost mesmerizing quality to his tawny eyes. "Is it?"

"You know it is!" she retorted, fighting back the angry tears. "I don't want to go with you. You're taking me against my will! And if that isn't kidnapping, I don't know what is. I could send you to jail for life for this!"

"Could you?" The cruel line of his mouth quirked crookedly.

"If you don't let go of my wrist, I'll scream. I'll scream so loud the whole town will hear me," Jacquie threatened. "I'll tell them what you're doing."

"No one will believe you," Choya taunted. "Not after I've already paid for the repairs to your car and for your motel room because of your misfortune in losing your wallet. They'll simply be astounded that you could be so ungrateful for all I've done."

"They'll believe me," she returned, "when I tell them the way you want me to pay you back."

"Idle words," he jeered, "with no proof to back them up. You can't cry rape because I haven't touched you. You could say that's what I planned, but it would be your word against mine. Who do you think they would believe?''

Jacquie flipped the hair away from her face, her hand trembling. He was right. She was a stranger and Choya was a member of the community, well known and respected from what she had seen.

"You won't get away with this entirely," she declared slowly. "Afterward—" a tight lump entered her throat at what would happen before the "afterward." "Afterward, I won't slink away. I'll tell everyone how you raped me and kept me prisoner. They'll believe me then."

"I can't argue with that," he agreed complacently. "Of course, then you'll have to prove that you were an unwilling participant. A lot of people have seen you playing up to my son before you lost your money. I can always call Bob as a witness concerning the way you all but propositioned him. The judge would take one look at you and know that you're not a shy, retiring little flower. Besides, you know you won't be unwilling."

Paling, Jacquie turned away from the wicked glitter in his eyes, biting into her trembling lower lip. Silently she swore at him, but she didn't say any of the expletives aloud.

Choya would only laugh at the impotency of her anger.

Retaining his grip on her wrist, he started the jeep with his left hand and reversed out of the parking lot. Not until they had turned off the highway onto a dusty gravel road winding into the mountains did he release his hold.

Massaging her throbbing wrist and hand, Jacquie stared at the desolate scenery through the dust cloud kicked up by the jeep. None of this could be happening to her. It was only a nightmare, if she could just wake up.

The jeep bounced over the little-traveled road. The bone-jarring ride would have wakened her if she had been asleep. The road twisted and curved along the foot of the mountains. Here and there along a mountain slope was the telltale scar of an abandoned mine.

Occasionally Jacquie glimpsed a derelict building, long deserted, or a rutted track leading away from the main road. Sometimes there was a small sign on a fence post, giving the name of a ranch. Mainly it was an endless landscape of sage and cactus and sunbaked rocks.

And dust. Swirling dust entered the open sides of the jeep to deposit a floury film on everything. The gritty particles powdered her face and skin and covered her clothes. Jacquie longed to ask how far they still had to go, certain the dust would suffocate her if she had to endure the ride much longer. But the silence was not one that she wanted to break.

When she had viewed the Dragoon Mountains from Boothill Cemetery, the deceiving distances of the desert had made them seem so close. Now Jacquie realized that Choya's ranch was miles from civilization. Any hope of escaping on foot was nullified by the undulating land which promised that a novice would be lost within minutes.

The jeep bounced off the road onto a rutted track seemingly leading to nowhere. Jacquie knew Choya was taking her to a prison where iron bars were not needed, nor locks and keys. For the first time in her life, she cursed her cockiness and the impetuous, wild streak that had got her into a situation that neither guile nor intelligence could get her out of.

When there seemed to be nothing on the horizon but desert scrub, unexpectedly large, light shapes took form. One was a house, low and sprawling with a wide, overhanging roof and stuccoed walls. The other was a similarly constructed building with a fenced enclosure extending from it.

Two large cottonwood trees shaded the west side of the house. Varieties of cacti instead of evergreen shrubs decorated the front yard. It couldn't be called a lawn since there was no grass, only more desert sand and rock.

Strangely Jacquie discovered she liked the ascetic purity and usage of desert growth to landscape the yard. Green grass and flowering shrubs would have been incongruous against the barren backdrop. Then she realized she was admiring the place that was to be her prison until Choya decided that her debt to him was paid.

As the jeep was braked to a silent stop in front of the house, the dust cloud caught up with it and rolled thickly in the open sides. Jacquie choked and began coughing. The strangling dust made it easy to summon bitterness to her voice.

"How can you live in such a godforsaken hole!" she exclaimed hoarsely.

Other than a sliding glance in her direction, Choya didn't acknowledge her remark at all. Stepping out of the jeep, he reached in back for her suitcase and handbag, tossing the latter to Jacquie. She barely caught it before the contents spilled.

"Get out," he ordered crisply.

"No." She wasn't going to walk into that house like a meek, sacrificial lamb.

Malicious laughter glinted in his eyes. "Do you expect me to carry you over the threshold like a virginal bride?"

"No," Jacquie retaliated. "I expected you to throw me over your shoulder and carry me inside like the barbaric savage that you are!" Her fingers had a death grip on her bag, the only weapon she seemed to have outside of a venomous tongue.

"I can do that." Choya glanced pointedly at the discoloring marks beginning to appear on her wrist. "But I wouldn't like to damage the goods any more than I have to before I use them."

An inferno of heat rushed through her body at his innuendo. "You're revolting!" she spat as she scrambled from the jeep, well aware that he would resort to physical force if he had to. The time to fight him was later, not now. He met her at the front of the jeep, blocking her path to the house. Steel fingers clamped onto her chin, twisting her face upward. Her turquoise eyes blazed with an inner fire.

"Revolting, am I?" he mocked harshly, then crushed her mouth with his.

Before Jacquie could attempt to struggle, he was setting her free. Furious, she wiped her mouth with the back of her hand, glaring at him even as her senses flamed to life.

Choya watched the conflicting reaction and smiled in satisfaction.

The front door of the house opened, and Jacquie eyed the tall, gaunt man standing in the shadow of the building's overhang. His angular features had a rough look, sharp edges that not even the weight of years on his shoulders had blunted. The leathered skin on his face was crisscrossed with wrinkles and his eyes were a piercing pale blue.

Choya had half turned at the sound of the door. Now his hand was gripping Jacquie's elbow and propelling her forward. The man's gaze sliced to him after making a thorough study of Jacquie. Choya stopped near the cement slab in front of the door.

"Sam, this is Jacqueline Grey," Choya spoke clearly and distinctly. "She's going to keep house for us for a while." His tawny eyes shifted to her wary expression. "Miss Grey, this is my father, Sam Barnett."

Except for his ruggedness, there was nothing about the older man that reminded Jacquie of his autocratic son. With a rush, she remembered the service-station mechanic explaining that Sam Barnett had found Choya as a day-old baby abandoned in a cactus patch, had reared him and later legally adopted him.

There was something forthright about the older man that brought a glimmer of hope to Jacquie. Her lips relaxed their tight line as she searched the lined face.

"That isn't exactly true, Mr. Barnett," she asserted. "Your son wants me here for a reason other than what he's given."

Sam Barnett looked her up and down, a roguish light suddenly brightening his blue eyes. "Dammit, he wouldn't be a man if he didn't!" he grinned. "If I was forty years younger—hell, if I was twenty years younger, I'd be chasin' you around the house right now." The smile lessened at Jacquie's wince. "You'll have to excuse my language, miss. I'm used to havin' men around. I do try to watch my language around the boy, though." His eyes narrowed slightly. "You aren't from around here, are you?"

"No." She shook her head, feeling truly defeated.

"Miss Grey is from Texas," Choya inserted. "She was in Tombstone having some repairs done to her car when her wallet with all her money was lost. She's here temporarily until she's earned enough for her bills and traveling money."

It all sounded so pat, so easily believed. If she tried to denounce what Choya was saying, it would sound like a wild tale. No one would believe her until it was too late.

"Well," Sam Barnett breathed in deeply, "I suppose I better start sweepin' out that room behind the kitchen. Got some clean sheets in the linen closet. Have to take a pillow from Robbie's bed."

The last statements were mumbled to himself as he made a verbal list of the things that needed to be done. He pivoted with difficulty, leaning heavily on a cane that Jacquie just noticed in his right hand. Awkwardly he hobbled into the house, depending on the cane for support.

Choya's hand pushed her forward into the house. Jacquie walked into an austerely furnished living room. A blackened fireplace was on the far outside wall. The long sofa was covered with a Navajo patterned blanket, the only vivid color in the room. Two large chairs sat opposite it, one with a footstool and reading lamp beside it. A rolltop desk was against one wall where rows of shelves were lined with books. Oak floors gleamed satin smooth. For a male household, everything was surprisingly clean and tidy.

A white-walled hallway branched off to the left from the living room, but Choya indicated that Jacquie should follow the rusty gray head of his father. The short hallway he took led into the kitchen.

The room was dominated by a large, painted wood table in the center with a red-checked oilcloth on its top. The wood cupboards were old and painted white and a large porcelain sink gaped in a yellowing countertop. The refrigerator was modern, but the gas stove had to be an antique. The floor was linoleum covered and continued in a short stretch to an outside door.

In between the back of the kitchen and the outside door was a second door. It was this door that was Sam Barnett's destination. Leaning on his cane, he pushed it open and waited for Jacquie.

"It isn't much," he said, "but it gives you some privacy from the rest of the house."

By that, Jacquie guessed that he meant the bedrooms were at the opposite end of the house. She darted a sideways glance at Choya, thinking for an instant that his plans might be foiled.

Nothing in his bronze mask revealed any displeasure at the location of her room. With a sinking heart, she realized that he considered its distance from the others an advantage. It was unlikely that a struggle would be heard.

The room was small. A double bed sat in one corner, taking up most of the floor space not occupied by a chest of drawers, a metal closet and a straight-backed chair. A plain, gold throw rug was on the floor in front of the bed. It was a starkly simple room, serving its purpose without any attempt to please the eye.

Choya walked into the room and laid her suitcase on the bed. "You can unpack," he said. "I'll bring the rest of your things this afternoon when I pick up your car." Then turning to the tall, gaunt man looking in, he said, "I won't be home for lunch, Sam."

A silent message must have accompanied his statement, because the older man nodded and limped away from the doorway. Jacquie tensed, wary now that Choya apparently wanted to see her alone. She decided it was better to attack before he had the chance.

"Your father is expecting me to do the housework," she accused.

"Is there anything wrong with that?" countered Choya. "It's a way to work out your room and board. Unless, of course, you'd rather work out that particular debt in the same way you'll be paying for the other."

"Don't be disgusting!"

"Disgusting, revolting—surely you can think of more original adjectives?" His mouth curved without humor. "I'm going into town now. If you have any thoughts of trying to run away while I'm gone, I advise you to forget them, I would simply find you and bring you back."

"I despise you," Jacquie muttered, wondering what she had ever found attractive about the man. But she knew very well how dangerously compelling he still was to her.

"Why?" he taunted. "Because after all these years of calling the tune, you finally have to pay the fiddler?"

On that profound question, he walked out of the room, leaving Jacquie shaking with unvoiced anger.

CHAPTER SIX

FUMING, JACQUIE turned toward the suitcase, resting her hands on top of it. If she tried to leave, she knew he would come after her. Frustration curled her fingers into fists. It was a duty to herself to try, but how? Sam Barnett limped to the doorway of her room. Instead of his cane, he was using a straw broom for support. Fighting to get a grip on her composure, Jacquie could only manage a sideways glance at him as he began awkwardly pushing the broom around on the tiled floor.

"I'll do that," she said tightly, unable to stand idly while the elderly man, practically crippled with arthritis, cleaned her room.

He hesitated, then handed her the broom. "I been doin' all this for so many years, it's going to seem strange havin' someone else do the work." He didn't hurry out of the room. "Fact is, Choya's wife—she died several years ago—she left most of the housework to me. And my own Gladys had been gone for over thirty-six years. This house hasn't known a woman to take care of it, nor have the people in it. I guess it don't look like much.''

"It's a very nice home." It was on the tip of Jacquie's tongue to tell him that she was being held a prisoner here, but what was the use?

"I'll go fetch the sheets." Sam Barnett turned, keeping a balancing hand on the wall, and limped from the room.

Jacquie stood for silent seconds, then began sweeping the room. She had completed that and was stoically unpacking her suitcase when Sam returned with the clean bed sheets. He stayed, keeping up a steady monologue of his first years on the ranch. At appropriate spots, Jacquie made the suitable responses, wondering all the while if Choya had told him not to leave her alone.

When she was finished, he showed her the part of the house that she hadn't seen. She found nothing unexpected. All the rooms were plain and serviceable. Then it was back to the kitchen where he suggested a cold lunch, explaining that his appetite wasn't what it used to be.

Jacquie was relieved. She was hungry, but doubted that the nervous churning of her stomach would let a heavy meal stay down.

He instructed her in the location of the various foods, utensils and dishes.

There was very little on her plate, but she managed to get it down. Sam offered to help with the washing up, but Jacquie declined—not out of any belief that it wasn't a man's place, but because she hoped he would leave the kitchen and allow her an opportunity to think in silence. He stayed, reaffirming her belief that he was acting on Choya's orders.

How could she ever get away when Choya had his father acting as a watchdog in his absence? It didn't matter that she didn't have the means of transportation to leave nor the exact knowledge of where to go. What mattered was the lack of opportunity to try.

After she had finished, Sam explained the household schedule; when the meals were eaten, the shopping was done, the clothes were washed and various rooms in the house were cleaned. Jacquie paid little attention to any of it, although she pretended to listen.

Her nerves were taut and raw, as finely drawn as a bowstring. The sound of a vehicle pulling to a stop outside the house sent her heart leaping. Her gaze flew to the wall clock above the refrigerator. It couldn't possibly be late afternoon already!

"That must be Choya," Sam commented, turning toward the archway to the living room.

At the opening of the front door, Jacquie half rose out of the kitchen chair, wanting to flee and not knowing where to go. There was the rapid thumping of crutches on the polished wood floor of the living room before Robbie burst into the kitchen, his face aglow with excitement.

"Jacquie!" He rushed forward almost faster than his crutches could propel him. "Dad said you were here, but I couldn't hardly believe him. Jacquie, I'm so glad you didn't leave!"

Certain that any second Robbie would pitch headlong to the floor, Jacquie stepped away from the chair, reaching out with her arms to catch him. He practically threw himself into them, discarding the crutches with a crash to wrap his arms around her middle in a fierce hug.

It was such a completely uninhibited and genuine embrace that Jacquie couldn't help responding to it. She returned his hug, the boy's warmth easing the cold fear that gripped her.

Robbie tipped his head back, pale brown eyes earnestly studying her. "Are you really going to stay? Dad said you were."

The smile on her lips became hesitant as she loosened his grip and bent down to his level. Her hands trembled on his shoulders. How could she possibly tell this little boy that she couldn't leave his home soon enough?

"Only... only for a while," she answered.

He must have sensed her reluctance. He wrapped his small arms around her neck, clinging to her in desperation as he buried his head against her shoulder.

"I hope you stay forever and ever," Robbie declared in a throbbing voice.

Instinctively, Jacquie smoothed the silken top of his head, brushing a light kiss on the area. She was drawn to the boy as inexplicably as she was drawn to his father. A tightness gripped her throat.

Out of the corner of her eye, she glimpsed a slight movement near the entrance to the living room. Her gaze swerved to investigate, encountering the muscled frame of Choya. Even in stillness, he possessed a vitality, a charged aura that seemed to crackle about him.

Tawny eyes held her paralyzed look, impassively studying her and the boy clutching her so possessively. Nothing in the chiseled granite features revealed any portion of his thoughts. There was no indication of how long he had been standing there nor how much he had overheard.

Shaken by the discovery of his presence, Jacquie slowly untangled Robbie's arms from around her neck, keeping a supporting hand at his waist while she retrieved his crutches. Ignoring Choya was difficult as she smiled at the boy.

"Have you seen my room?" Robbie asked eagerly. "I have a whole bunch of Indian arrowheads. Gramps and me, we go looking for them. Now you can come along, too."

"Of course," Jacquie agreed weakly.

"And I want to show you my horse, too. I have one of my very own," he declared proudly, again brimming with excitement. "No one else can ride him except me—Dad said so. I'll let you ride him, though. I can't ride him until I get my cast off. Can you ride a horse, Jacquie?"

"Not very well," she admitted, since her horseback riding had been limited to an occasional outing with a group to a local stable.

"I'll teach you." He shifted his crutches. "Come on, I'll show you my horse. His name is Apache. This all used to be Apache land, did you know that?"

"Yes, I did."

"Save your tour for later, Robbie," Choya ordered. "You have to change out of your school clothes and do your chores first."

Robbie gave his father an impatient glance and turned back to Jacquie. "We're going to have a lot of fun together. After I get my cast off, we can go riding together over some of the same trails that Cochise and Geronimo rode. And there's this place by a waterhole where Gramps and I find our arrowheads. We can swim there, too, and have picnics and—"

"Robbie," Choya's low voice firmly interrupted his son, "Jacquie isn't here to be your playmate."

With her temper seething near boiling point, Jacquie straightened, the fiery sparkle of battle in her eyes as she met the gold mask of his gaze.

"Did you forget to tell Robbie that I was your playmate, not his?" she challenged.

The thin line of Choya's mouth tightened ominously. Confused by Jacquie's sudden bitterness, Robbie glanced bewilderedly from her to his glowering father. The brittle silence was broken by the soft chuckle of Sam Barnett.

"I was beginning to think that girl had no spirit at all." His blue eyes twinkled as he glanced at Choya. "She's barely said one sentence to me since you left."

There was a visible relaxing of the hard set of Choya's features, a glitter of lazy amusement in the eyes that swept over Jacquie before moving to his son.

"Go and change your school clothes, Robbie," Choya repeated in a calmly chiding tone.

Robbie hesitated. "What did Jacquie mean?"

"It's nothing for you to worry about," was the even reply.

The answer apparently satisfied the boy. With an I'll-see-you-later smile to Jacquie, he thumped out of the kitchen in the direction of his bedroom. Sam Barnett gripped his cane and pushed himself from the chair.

"I didn't get my afternoon nap," he announced. "I think I'll lay down for an hour before dinner."

Stubbornly, Jacquie maintained her challenging stance, refusing to relent an inch although she had been left alone with Choya. If anything her anger increased. She held his gaze with unwavering defiance.

"Did you tell your father the way you're planning to have me repay you?" she accused lowly.

"No." He moved leisurely into the kitchen. "Did you want me to?"

She couldn't shake the eerie sensation that she was being stalked.

"No!" she hissed, and spun away, clasping her hands in front of her.

"Then why did you ask?" Choya questioned smoothly.

"Because he didn't leave me alone for a second," she snapped, turning her profile to him without glancing around.

"If he had, what would you have done?" He stopped behind her, his head drawn back, increasing the effect that he was looking down at her.

"I would have run!" Jacquie retorted.

"Even knowing I would come after you?"

"Knowing that would make me run faster." She tossed her head back, staring determinedly ahead. The awareness that he towered behind her had quickened her breathing to an agitated rate.

His fingers closed over her arm to turn her around. Jacquie obeyed willingly, lashing out with her free hand at his sun-browned cheek. Her open palm didn't reach its target as his lightning reflexes had his other hand checking the swing in mid-flight. Brutally he twisted her arm behind her back, arching her rigid body against his.

At the involuntary flash of fear in her eyes, he laughed softly, almost silently. "Are you afraid I might decide to make love to you now?" The grooves deepened around his mouth as he mocked, "Anticipation, remember? I shall enjoy waiting and watching you wonder if it will be tonight, tomorrow, the day after or even longer.''

A gasp of protest and dread filled her lungs as he set her away from him as quickly as he had captured her. It was a chilling sentence. The punishment would be mental as well as physical and she was helpless.

Before Choya could consider changing his mind, Jacquie ordered her weak legs to carry her from the kitchen. He didn't try to stop her. He must have guessed that she was only running from his presence and not attempting to escape.

Too shattered to go far, she ended up in her small bedroom off the kitchen. There was no lock on the door, so she quickly slid the straight-backed chair beneath the knob. As she moved away, there was a knock on the door and she froze.

''I'm going to do chores,'' Choya stated, not even testing the doorknob to see if it would open. ''Have dinner ready in an hour.''

Striding footsteps carried him away, followed by the slam of the outside door. Jacquie stood in the center of the room, huddling in despair. Then she realized that that was what he wanted her to do. He wanted her to be on tenterhooks, to turn her into a quivering mass of nerves.

Jacquie raised her chin. She would never bow her head to any man, least of all Choya Barnett. She had fled from him for the last time. He might take her, but he would never find any satisfaction.

There was a laundry room and small bathroom across from her bedroom. Jacquie used it to splash cold water on her face. The reviving chill was just what she needed to bolster her resolve as she entered the kitchen. The secret would be to not let her mind dwell on the reason she was in the house. She banished all thought of it as she concentrated on the menu for the evening meal. Never much of a cook, she kept it simple—fried chops, potatoes, a vegetable and a salad. The stove proved to be a worthy opponent to her effort, cantankerously refusing to light, then stubbornly resisting her attempts to regulate the flame.

Finally the potatoes were boiling and the chops were in the iron skillet and the vegetable was in a pan waiting to be heated. Jacquie felt secure that she could leave the food to cook while she fixed the cabbage salad.

As she was nearly finished tossing the canned milk, spices and sugar with the chopped cabbage, she heard a sizzling hiss from the stove. A quick glance saw the lid of the potato pan bouncing while boiling water bubbled down the side. At the same instant, she noticed smoke rising from the skillet.

Grabbing a pot holder from the drawer, she dashed to the old black and white stove, hesitating over which to rescue first. Deciding on the potatoes, she leaned forward to reach the pan on the rear burner. Her long hair fell forward. The outside door slammed, followed by footsteps. "What are you doing?" Choya demanded.

Jacquie checked her movement to dart him a quick glance, then reverted her attention to the pan. "The potatoes are boiling over," she stated crisply.

An iron band circled her waist, lifting her off her feet and simultaneously pushing her away from the stove. She staggered backward at his abrupt release as he took the pot holder from her hand and set the pan aside.

"Don't you know you can catch your hair on fire leaning across a stove like that?" he glowered. "Especially when it's as long as yours!"

"I didn't think," Jacquie breathed, then glanced at the stove. The smoke was really billowing from the skillet now. "The meat!" she exclaimed.

Choya turned, wrapping the pot holder around the handle and lifting the skillet from the fire. Quickly he shut off the burner before setting it back down. With a fork, he turned over the chops, revealing the charred sides. His glance at Jacquie spoke volumes.

"I never claimed to be a cook," she defended herself from his silent condemnation.

He lifted the lid on the pan of potatoes and a vague scent of something scorched filled the air. She brushed a hand across her forehead.

"All you had to do was turn the heat down," Choya said dryly.

"That's easy to say," she protested, feeling his criticism was unwarranted. "That stove is an antique. Only my grandmother would know how it works."

"Sam doesn't have any trouble with it."

"Which proves he's as old as my grandmother!" Jacquie retorted.

There was a glint of laughter in his eyes, then he turned toward the stove. "Come here. Let me show you how it works."

Ignoring the tingle that danced down her spine at standing so close to him, Jacquie listened attentively to his instructions. He spoke clearly and concisely, sliding a mocking glance at her only when he had finished.

"Now see what you can do about salvaging the meal while I wash up," he ordered.

"I'll try," she sighed, and poked a fork into the pork chops to see how badly they were ruined.

As Choya started to walk away, a faint smile curving the hard mouth, Robbie hobbled into the kitchen. He halted just inside the room and sniffed the air, wrinkling his nose in distaste.

"What's that?" he frowned warily.

"Dinner," Choya replied with a glittering look at Jacquie. "Or perhaps it's a burnt offering." Her cheeks flamed at his laughing taunt. "Come on, son," he said. "Let's wash our hands."

It definitely wasn't the tastiest meal Jacquie had ever prepared, although her experience in the culinary arts was very limited. There hadn't been another comment from Choya or Robbie, but Sam had clicked his tongue in dismay at the sight of the blackened pork chops.

The minor disaster meant that Jacquie had to spend more time than normal cleaning up, since the stove had to be scoured where the potatoes had boiled over. Then Robbie had appeared in the kitchen when she had finished. A checkerboard was in his hand and he challenged her to a game.

"I'm an expert," he declared, and proceeded to beat her soundly. When he proposed a second game, Jacquie suggested it was time for him to be in bed. "Okay," Robbie agreed without argument. "We can play another game tomorrow night. Don't feel bad that I beat you. I been playing checkers since I was three. Dad is teaching me chess, but I'm not very good at it, yet."

Jacquie smiled and said that chess was a complicated game. Silently considering the way Choya had outmaneuvered her so many times, she was certain he was a master at the game.

At Robbie's request, she tucked him into bed, then left his room when Choya appeared to wish him good-night. It wasn't a hasty retreat she made, keeping a firm hold of her resolve not to run from him.

As she entered her own bedroom, she congratulated herself on offering him such a calm good-night when she had walked past him. She had felt his tawny eyes briefly narrow on her, no doubt measuring the thickness of her composure.

Yawning, she didn't particularly care that for the moment it was vulnerably thin. She undressed for bed, crawling beneath the covers with the half-formed plan of waking after a few hours' sleep and attempting to steal from the house in the middle of the night.

Never would she cower before Choya nor beg for mercy. But she would take advantage of any opportunity to escape. Escaping a prison was not the same thing as fleeing from her jailer, she assured herself.

Within minutes of her head touching the pillow, she was asleep. Mental exhaustion made it a dreamless state and her subconscious failed to waken her in the midnight hours to escape.

A hand gripped her shoulder, shaking it slightly. Jacquie tried to shrug it away and snuggle deeper beneath the covers. The hand tightened.

"Rise and shine," a voice said.

"Go away," she mumbled sleepily without opening her eyes. Then memory returned as to where she was and who had just spoken. She rolled onto her back, automatically drawing the covers over her breasts. The gray light of dawn was peering through the window as she focused her somewhat bleary gaze on Choya.

She choked back the impulse to order him from her room, and asked instead, "What do you want?" An equally foolish question, since she didn't really want to know the answer.

Still drugged from heavy sleep, her senses were slow to alertness. Every part of him that her guarded look saw indicated his freshness and overwhelming vitality. Half-closed eyes of shimmering sand gold returned the study with disturbing results.

"You have twenty minutes to get up, get dressed if you choose, and have my breakfast on the table," Choya stated.

Jacquie breathed in deeply, relief flowing through her tensed muscles. He was still playing his waiting game and trying to turn her into a slave who did his bidding.

He wasn't her master because she wasn't his slave. Pulling the covers over her shoulders, she turned onto her side away from him.

"Fix your own breakfast," she muttered, and nestled her head deeply in the pillow.

The covers were ripped away and the soft flesh of her arm seized in a punishing grip. In a fluid motion, she was rolled onto her back, her other arm gripped, and half lifted out of the bed. When the movement stopped, she was drawn close to his face, her feet twisted in the bed sheets.

The strap of her pale blue shortie nightgown had slipped from her shoulder, revealing the rounded swell of her breast. The blocking grip of Choya's hand kept the strap from sliding farther and revealing more.

Deliberately he studied what the gown exposed, his gaze wandering to the pulsing vein in her neck, then on to the softness of her lips parted in surprise. His glittering eyes skimmed over the alluring disarray of her hair and halted his inspection with the turquoise pools of her rounded eyes.

Jacquie's hands rested on the solidness of his waist. With her feet tangled in the covers, she had no leverage to struggle. The touch of her hands against him was more for support than any thought to fight him.

The male line of his mouth descended to play with her lips, teasing the way they trembled at his touch. It was an exquisite kind of torture for Jacquie, afraid to feel the branding hardness of a kiss of possession yet unable to make herself twist away to avoid it. The scent of him enveloped her with the intoxicating effects of a heady liquor.

"If you don't get up and fix my breakfast," his warm breath flowed over her skin as he spoke against her lips, "I may decide to have it in bed."

"I can't." Her lips quivered against his teasing mouth.

Motionless for an instant, Choya asked, "Why?"

"Because—" Jacquie breathed shakily, his disturbing attraction almost more than she could cope with in this semi-languorous state "—I can't get up until you let go of me."

Lazily he drew his head back, dark hair glistening in the artificial light. Cat-soft eyes shimmered over her face, almost physically touching each feature before they glittered with a seductive light.

With deliberate slowness, he laid her back on the bed. Then he bent over her, a hand resting on the mattress on either side of her. Jacquie swallowed, trying not to reveal her lack of composure or her rising fear.

"You're free," he mocked. "You can get up and get dressed now."

She hesitated, uncertain that he meant what he said. To get up meant to move past him. The question was would he let her by? Yet she was positive if she didn't try, he would interpret it as an invitation.

With a quailing heart, she lifted her head from the pillow. As she moved upward, Choya straightened with a taunting gleam in his eye. Temper flashed in her eyes that he should toy with her so, but Jacquie didn't release it. She moved swiftly away from the bed, hurrying to her clothes on the straight chair.

When she glanced over her shoulder, Choya was leaning against the door frame, his arms folded across his waist. He looked as if he planned to stay.

"Will you please leave my room so I can dress?" Jacquie made the demand in a wary tone.

"Don't mind me," Choya drawled. "Go right ahead."

Seething inwardly, she wanted to order him out at the top of her lungs, but something in the veiled alertness of his gaze said he was waiting for that. With a nonchalance that she was far from feeling, she shrugged and turned her back to him.

Without removing her nightgown, she slipped on the faded jeans. The action gave him an unlimited view of naked thigh and leg, but that was all. With the front of her denims fastened securely, Jacquie pulled the nightgown over her head.

The cascading waves of her silvery blond hair covered her creamy gold shoulders as she kept her back squarely toward him. With an economy of movement she pulled on a strawberry-colored knit top and turned around.

There was an arrogant arch to one of her curved brows.

"What would you like for breakfast?" she inquired with false solicitude.

There was a half smile on his mouth as he straightened from the door. "Whatever you fix is fine." And he walked from the room.

CHAPTER SEVEN

THE KEYS weren't in her car. The maze of wires didn't give her a clue as to how it could be started without the ignition key. Sighing in defeat, she stepped from the car and closed the door.

A hot breeze blew from the south; whirling dust devils sprang up to dance through the sage and cactus growth, then spun themselves out and disappeared. The afternoon sun burned over the bareness of her arms. There was no sign of activity from the house. Jacquie crossed her fingers that it meant Sam Barnett was still sleeping. This was her third day of being Choya's prisoner and her first opportunity to test the strength of the invisible bars of her cage.

Yesterday she had steered the talkative Sam Barnett into discussing the land surrounding the ranch. Scanning the countryside, she realized he had told her very little that would be useful. His information had been historical.

To the north was the virtually impregnable stronghold of Cochise. Beyond it was Apache Pass. To the southwest lay Tombstone. The nearest neighboring ranch was to the south.

Everywhere Jacquie looked, she saw the savage beauty of the Sonora desert. She was not yet so desperate to escape that she wanted to flee on foot. The keys to her car were obviously in Choya's possession.

Sighing a second time, she hooked her thumbs in the belt loops of her black slacks. The metal of the silver concho belt was warm against her fingers. A horse whinnied near the barn and she wandered toward the sound.

At the corral, she rested her forearms on the upper bar and the toe of her shoe on the lowest. Three horses were in the enclosure. At the sight of Jacquie, they snorted and trotted nervously to the far end.

With the car eliminated and Jacquie unwilling to risk walking, that left escaping on horseback. Her mouth curved wryly. The first problem would be catching a horse; the second would be saddling him. She hadn't the vaguest notion how to go about doing either. At the riding stable, the horses had always been saddled and tied to a post.

So far, the invisible bars seemed escape-proof. Somewhere there had to be a vulnerable spot. Jacquie's concern was that she was running out of time to find it. Choya hadn't made any attempt to carry out his threat, but that didn't mean he wouldn't.

The horses pricked their ears and faced the rutted track leading to the ranch yard. Jacquie turned, stepping away from the corral when she recognized the school bus bringing Robbie home. She walked forward to meet him as the bus stopped.

When the doors swished open, Robbie greeted her silently with a wide grin. He paused at the steps to glance over his shoulder at the other children in the bus, school papers tucked under his arm as he rested on the crutches.

"See?" Jacquie heard his voice challenge. "I told you!"

It was a curious and cryptic statement.

He maneuvered the crutches and the unwieldy cast on his leg down the steps. His movement was awkward because Robbie was more concerned that he would drop his school papers than he was that he might fall.

"Let me carry your papers," Jacquie offered when he was safely on the ground.

As Robbie handed them to her, she noticed the bus driver give her a curious look and nod. Then the doors were closing and the bus was turning to leave. There had been something more than mere surprise in the driver's expression. Jacquie glanced warily at Robbie.

"What was all that about in the bus?" she asked.

"Nobody believed me when I told them you were living with us," he answered, starting toward the house. "When they saw you, they knew I was telling the truth."

Oh, great, Jacquie thought to herself. The whole town would know she was out here and believe she was staying of her own free will. The bars closed more securely around her.

"What did you tell them about me?" she questioned.

Robbie seemed to hesitate. "Just that you were staying with us."

Her finger encountered the smooth finish of a stiff paper amongst the other plain papers in her hand. Curious, Jacquie separated it from the others and found herself looking at an enlarged photograph of a smiling young woman with short, cornsilk-colored hair—Robbie's mother. She had seen the picture in his room, framed and sitting on a table by his bed.

"Why did you take this to school, Robbie?" Jacquie eyed him suspiciously.

He peered at her anxiously through the top of his lashes, his pale golden hair gleaming brightly in the sun. "I took that one so I could show them what you looked like." He hastened to add, "You're prettier than any of the other mothers."

"You didn't tell them I was your mother, did you?"

Robbie looked uncomfortable. "No."

Jacquie sensed it was a truthful answer and also that it wasn't the whole truth. "Do they think I'm your mother?"

"Well, maybe some of them do," he conceded.

"And you didn't tell them any different?" she accused with a heavy sigh. His chin dipped toward his chest. "Robbie, I am not your mother. I am not even your stepmother. It wasn't right for you to let the rest of your classmates think that I am."

"I know," he mumbled.

"Tomorrow you'll have to tell them the truth."

Large, luminous brown eyes were turned to her. "I wish you were my mother."

It was such an expressively voiced statement that Jacquie lost her irritation. Kneeling beside him, she gazed into his plaintively wistful face.

"You know it's not possible," she smiled gently.

"Why?" Robbie asked solemnly. "Why couldn't I pretend that you're my mother? There wouldn't be anything wrong with that."

"Oh, Robbie," Jacquie sighed, wishing she was more immune to his innocent charm.

"It would just be pretend between you and me. I wouldn't tell anybody else," he persisted as he saw her weakening.

"I—" She shook her head hopelessly. "Pretend. Just between you and me. And everybody else would know that I'm not your mother."

"I promise." He leaned heavily on one crutch and crossed his heart with one finger.

"Okay." Jacquie offered her hand to seal the agreement.

Robbie shook it eagerly. "Can I call you mom? When we're alone, I mean," he qualified quickly.

"Only when we're alone," she agreed. It was only a game.

She had played "pretend" often as a child. It couldn't do any harm.

His eyes twinkled brightly as a beaming smile split his face from ear to ear. "I'm hungry, mom," he declared.

Jacquie laughed and straightened, trailing a hand over his shoulders. "Then let's go in the house and see what we can find to eat."

Their secret game kept Robbie bubbling with an inner excitement all the rest of the afternoon and into the evening. Every time he looked at Jacquie when his grandfather and Choya were around, she read the silent message of "mother" in his eyes. His delight was such that she couldn't bring herself to feel guilty for allowing him to become more attached to her.

The evening meal could not have been classified as a success. Although Choya had shown her how to operate the stove, Jacquie still had difficulty judging the amount of heat for cooking. Tonight it had been the corn that was scorched.

Sam, probably out of self-preservation, had offered several times to help with the meals, but Jacquie had steadfastly refused. Stubbornly she had insisted on cooking everything herself. Her unintentional failures were a means of getting back at Choya for blackmailing her into the role of housekeeper. She almost hoped that she never would learn how to operate the stove successfully, even if she did have to eat the ruined dishes along with everyone else.

Except for Choya's comment about a "burnt offering" the first time she had fixed a meal, he had made no remark about her substandard cooking ability. Tonight he had been even more silent than usual, but his tawny gaze had narrowed on her thoughtfully several times. Jacquie simply ignored him. She couldn't begin to guess the reason for his silence and she wasn't going to try.

After the dishes were washed and Robbie was tucked into bed, Jacquie avoided the living room where Choya and Sam were, in favor of her bedroom. She had decided that she had to make another attempt to appeal to her parents. It would require a carefully worded letter that would make them aware of the seriousness of her need without alarming them.

When she sat down to write the first draft, she found it was going to be more difficult than she had first thought. She was caught again in the same trap. If she told them about Choya's blackmail and threat and they came out here to rescue her from his villainous clutches, they would hear his false story that he had only offered her a job as his housekeeper so that she might earn the money to pay for her debts. And there wouldn't be any way for Jacquie to disprove his claim and many ways for him to prove it.

The several sheets of crumpled stationery in the wastebasket revealed her number of failures. Finally Jacquie crinkled up the last par-

tially written letter and threw it in the basket
with the others. A letter was not the answer.
Tomorrow while Sam was taking his afternoon nap, she would telephone them again,
and this time she wouldn't reverse the charges.

The house was silent as she stepped from her
room. She paused in the hall, glancing at her
watch. As impossible as it seemed, it was after
ten o'clock. The absence of any sound indicated that everyone else was in bed. She
walked across the small hall to the laundry
room and bathroom, piling her long hair on
top of her head and fastening it with two hair-
pins as she went.

A brisk shower chased away the tension and
frustrations that had built when she had been
trying to compose the letter. She still had no
idea what she would say when she talked to her
parents on the telephone, but she was confident she would think of something when the
time came.

With most of the water from the shower
spray wiped from her skin, she wrapped the
oversized bath towel around her and tucked
the fold securely. The terry cloth material
nearly reached the middle of her thighs, its soft
roughness warm against her skin.

Her cosmetics were on the shelf above the
sink. Reaching for a jar of moisturizing cream,

she removed the lid and began creaming her face. As she was working it into her forehead, the door opened and Choya walked in.

After a startled look, Jacquie took a hasty step in the direction of her clothes, then stopped. "You could have knocked," she said sharply, and dabbed more cream on her face.

"I could have," he agreed, walking over to stand by the sink where Jacquie was.

Unwillingly her gaze slid to the male reflection joining hers in the mirror. The ruggedly hewn features were unreadable as he watched her intently.

"What did you want?" Jacquie asked with studied indifference. She wished for the robe that was in her room, although its short length would not have offered much more cover than the towel did.

"It's been a long time since I've watched the nightly ablutions of a woman," Choya commented idly.

Her stomach began somersaulting nervously and she rubbed the cream more vigorously into her cheeks to give them some color. She didn't believe for one minute that was the reason for his visit, and she was afraid to guess what the real reason might be. She lowered her lashes to conceal the trepidation her expressive turquoise eyes might reveal. Devoid of darkening mascara, they lay long and thick, a light brown against her skin.

"Really?" she mocked in a sarcastically doubting tone.

Not for anything did she want him to know the way his nearness was disturbing her. The breadth of his shoulders silently intimidated, his height dwarfing her reflection.

Choya seemed to withdraw, watching her with an aloofness that was unnerving.

"Someone stopped me today to see if congratulations were in order. It seems there's a rumor circulating that I've remarried."

"I certainly didn't start the rumor," Jacquie denied crisply.

"You wouldn't happen to know who did, would you?" His tawny gold eyes had narrowed on her, glittering and dangerous.

"How could I?" she laughed bitterly. "I haven't spoken to anyone except you, your father and Robbie since you kidnapped me."

"And you don't think it's possible that one of them might have mentioned you?" Choya persisted.

The incident with Robbie was vividly recalled. The recollection must have flickered across her face, because his expression hardened.

"Of course it's possible," Jacquie hedged, reluctant to admit that Robbie had let his classmates believe that she was his new mother.

"It's even possible that my son has told his classmates and teacher about you in such a way that they might believe we're married, isn't it?" he taunted.

"I really don't know," she lied, shrugging one bare shoulder.

"If you did, you certainly wouldn't condone or encourage Robbie, would you?" The line of his jaw was set in a grimly forbidding line.

Nervously, Jacquie moistened her lips, wondering how much Choya actually knew and how much he was only guessing. She smoothed some of the moisturizing cream over the fine bridge of her nose.

"That's a silly question," she smiled as if it was too ludicrous to merit a reply.

"Then answer it," he challenged.

"Robbie is not the type of boy to lie or tell tales. He would never claim that I was his new mother when he knows that I'm not," Jacquie stated in an attempt to avoid a direct answer.

"Robbie claims that you agreed to be his pretend mother."

Jacquie took a slow, deep breath. "He did?" So much for the ability of little boys to keep secrets!

"Not willingly. He was very persistent in his denials until I confronted him with the questions his teacher asked me," Choya stated. "After that, he felt in the need of a total confession."

"It was a harmless game of pretend." She screwed the lid back on the jar of moisturizing cream.

"Harmless as far as you were concerned," he jeered cuttingly. "Robbie is just a little boy. You probably thought it was cute that he wanted to pretend you were his mother. It certainly wouldn't hurt you when the game was over. What do you care about the hurts of a small child?"

"It was just a game, nothing more," Jacquie protested. "Robbie knows I'm not his mother and never will be."

"He might say that. He might even believe it right now, but if the two of you keep playing this 'game'—" with sarcastic emphasis "—soon he will believe that it isn't just pretend."

Jacquie replaced the jar on the shelf and turned to face Choya. "In other words," she tipped her head to the side in a confident manner, "he'll become too attached to me.

That was one of the risks you took when you brought me out here, remember?''

He studied her for long, measuring seconds through half-closed eyes. "I underestimated you," he stated huskily. "I never believed that you would deliberately hurt my son to get back at me."

A muscle was twitching uncontrollably along his cheek. It had never been her intention, consciously or unconsciously, to use Robbie to punish Choya. To deny it would be a waste of energy. Choya would never believe that she genuinely liked his son.

If she couldn't fight him, she would join him. Robbie was obviously his vulnerable spot. She might as well try to make use of it while she had the chance.

"Robbie doesn't have to get hurt, you know." She blinked her sea-green eyes at him, keeping them round and blank of expression. "The game of pretend only started today. It can be stopped now before he begins to believe it."

"How?" A cynical brow arched doubtfully.

"It's very simple," she shrugged. "If you let me go, I'll leave Robbie alone. But if you continue to force me to stay here, I'll keep up this game of pretend. You can't watch me every

minute of the day. And Robbie will only start
to hate you if you try to come between us. You
give me my car and I'll give you back your
son.''

A smile of satisfaction curved the fullness of
her lips as Choya glared at her in a cold fury.
For once, she had him trapped. It could not
have worked out better if she had planned it.
The impulse to drive home her victory was too
great to resist.

"You think about it." She lightly patted a
lean cheek with the tips of her fingers.

Instantly her fingers were seized and crushed
together. Jacquie didn't attempt to free her
hand even though the grip was painful. Boldly
she met the savage fire in his gaze, a smug
gleam in her own eyes.

"You're trying to call the tune again without paying the fiddler, aren't you?" he
snarled. Jacquie's smile merely deepened, but
she didn't make a verbal response. "It's time
there was a demand for payment."

There was a second to blink at his unexpected declaration. In the next, she was being
swept off her feet, an arm pinned between her
body and his chest. The other was caught in
the vice of his circling grip. Blood hammered
in her ears, her breath taken away.

"Put me down!" Fear shook her voice.

Choya laughed harshly and kicked the hall door open wider. Jacquie twisted and strained against his hold, her feet flailing empty air in useless scissor motions as he carried her to the bedroom. The blue coverlet of her bed loomed ahead of her. She was dumped onto its darkness.

The mattress dipped beneath his joining weight. Jacquie opened her mouth to scream, but her cry was smothered by his mouth. She was trapped beneath the hard length of his body. Dizzying waves of fear washed through her, but she fought them back.

When her long fingernails began to dig into his muscled shoulders, her wrists were seized and arms forced above her head. The heat of his body consumed her flesh in hot flames while the musky scent of his maleness filled her lungs.

She tried to elude the bruising pressure of his mouth and almost succeeded as she twisted her face into the blue coverlet. Choya shifted slightly, letting one large hand hold her wrists, freeing the other to capture her chin.

"No!" Jacquie managed before his mouth closed over hers in angry possession.

Brutally he forced her throbbing lips open with his thumb, tasting the honeyed sweetness of her mouth with primitive passion. Her resistance wavered under his sensual assault. His savage lovemaking sparked an animal response within her, forcing her to struggle with herself as well as Choya.

With her efforts divided into two battle-fronts, her strength weakened. Alternately she fought his kiss and returned its fire. His hand slid from her chin along her throat and over the nakedness of her golden tan shoulders. The roughly sensual caress sent quivers down her spine.

Sensing it, Choya followed the trail of his hand, nibbling at the sensitive area below her ear lobe and the hollow of her shoulder. An unwilling sigh of delight escaped her lips. While his mouth continued its exploration of her pleasure points, his hand moved downward, encountered the protective towel and pulled at the tuck that held it in place.

Briefly the action revived Jacquie's will. "No," she protested. "Please, don't!"

In answer he lifted his head. Fascinating tawny eyes studied the reluctantly aroused expression on her face. The caressive light stole her breath as desert star fire flickered through the window to bronze his features.

Never had he seemed so stunningly male nor so disturbingly attractive as he did at that moment. He freed her wrists and lowered his hand to spread strong fingers through the molten silver of her hair.

"No?" His mouth quirked and began its descent.

As it mobilely captured hers in persuasive ardor, Jacquie brought her numbed hands down to press against his muscled arms. Then, almost of their own volition, they slid to the solidness of his back. The wildfire racing through her veins burned the last bridge of inhibition. The searing longing inside her for his possession was transmitted in the hungry response to her lips.

The crispness of his clothes was rough against her skin, yet its abrasive quality stimulated her nerve ends to a fever pitch of awareness. The beat of his heart was drumming to the tempo of her own.

When he moved away from her, Jacquie was still caught in the spell of his seductive touch. She was frozen, incapable of movement at the withdrawal of his body warmth. Every fiber pulsed with her need of him. Weakly, her lashes lifted.

"Choya," she whispered in an aching plea for him to return.

An arm slipped beneath her, hair rough against her skin as he half lifted her toward him. There was another movement, then she was being pressed back against the coolness of the sheets, the bed covers cast aside.

Afraid he would leave her again, she reached out to cling to him. Her hands slid around the rippling bareness of his shoulders, drawing him down. The fiery warmth of his skin melted away the last vestige of chill.

The hungry demand of his kiss removed the fear that he might leave her. Jacquie gloried in the knowledge, her breast swelling under his arousing touch. The world had spun away, leaving only the two of them in the universe.

The wild song in her heart was a rhapsody under his guidance. The intimate exploration of his hands provided the melody, the notes soaring to new unreached scales. It was an age-old tune that Jacquie was experiencing for the first time, the crash of cymbals shuddering through her with ecstasy. He was the master fiddler calling the tune and she was spinning and whirling and learning the new steps.

His lips opened warmly over hers. The tempo softened, its pagan beat leashed. In the momentary lull of sensation, Jacquie floated slowly back to the ground. The mindless bliss began drifting away. She closed her eyes tightly to shut out the reality—that she was actually inviting him to make love to her. She shivered against him when she failed to block out the knowledge. He gathered her more closely to him, brushing a rough kiss on the silken mass of hair near her ear.

Her hands violently pushed him away. "Leave me alone! Go away!" Her voice was hoarsely bitter with the loss of her self-pride.

Choya tensed as if to employ his superior strength and Jacquie held her breath.

At the shifting movement of his weight off the bed, her heart cried out for him to stay and to hold her tightly in his arms. Stiffly she stayed where he had left her, listening to his silent movements and holding back her pain until he had left the room.

One tear fell, then another. Finally there was a river of tears rushing down her cheeks to drench the pillow. She buried her face in its dampness to muffle her sobs.

CHAPTER EIGHT

HER EYES opened reluctantly. The full light of a morning sun streamed through the window. A gray lethargy dulled her senses. For an instant, she couldn't even remember where she was. She felt bruised and battered and didn't know why.

Throwing back the covers, she slid from the bed. A post offered support when her legs trembled weakly beneath her. Her dazed glance out the window focused on the shiny, spreading stalks of a cholla cactus. Choya. Memory contracted her stomach with sickening shame. She wanted to crawl beneath the covers and hide. For all her outcries denying his attraction, she had nearly succumbed to his advances last night—willingly.

Robotlike, Jacquie walked to the closet and chest of drawers, dressing without any particular concern about her appearance. She was indifferent to the lateness of the hour. There was no curiosity as to why she had been allowed to sleep so late, who had got the breakfast and seen Robbie onto the school bus.

Emptied of all feeling, she was hollow and insensitive. She walked back to the bed, shoving the blanket and bedspread to the foot, and began stripping the top sheet from the mattress.

Footsteps stopped outside her door. The knob turned to swing it open. Jacquie glanced over her shoulder, her blank gaze focusing on Choya framed by the doorway. Tall, vitally masculine, he paused there.

The light in his tawny eyes was one she had never seen before. Not that she cared. At this moment she didn't care about anything.

"I thought I heard you moving about," he said quietly. "I guessed—" his alert gaze swept appraisingly over her "—you would sleep late."

Jacquie turned her head away. "I'll fix breakfast shortly." Her voice was as flat as her spirit.

"There's no need. Sam took care of it," Choya replied.

Shrugging her lack of interest, she started tucking the ends of her shirt into her jeans. She was aware that he was still standing there watching her, and his presence disturbed her. Her nerve ends sharpened, focusing on Choya.

There could have been a mortal wound in her heart and she would have felt no pain.

His firm stride carried Choya toward her. Jacquie heard it, but determinedly kept her attention on her shirt. When he stopped behind her, she didn't acknowledge his nearness with a look.

His hands lightly gripped the sides of her waist, their touch unexpectedly paralyzing her for an instant. She didn't resist when he drew her back against the muscled hardness of his chest nor when his arms crossed around the front of her slender waist. Her hands hesitated away from her as she inhaled the lusty scent of his maleness, familiar and intoxicating.

Out of the corner of her eye, Jacquie saw the dark gleam of his brown hair. Then he buried his mouth along the side of her neck.

"Jacqueline." He said her name in a huskily caressing tone.

For an instant, she relaxed against him, finding solace and nourishment for the emptiness of last night. Just as suddenly she hated his tenderness. She hated him.

Last night he had nearly seduced her. He couldn't come here this morning and expect her to forgive. Not once did it occur to her that she had been a more than willing participant.

There was only cold hatred as she turned in his embrace. She wedged her arms against his chest, gaining distance from his bent head. The smoldering light of his gaze roamed possessively over her upturned face.

"If you'd warned me you were coming this morning, I would have worn my armory," she told him with chilling aloofness.

His head drew back sharply, his gaze narrowing to a piercing intensity. The jeweled brilliance of her eyes left Choya in little doubt of what she was feeling.

"Should I expect morning assaults as well as evening from now on?" Jacquie challenged when he remained silent.

"Dammit, Jacquie, I—" he began angrily.

"What do you have to swear about?" she interrupted, twisting free of his arms to glare at him indignantly. "It's a pity you didn't get your money's worth last night, you certainly tried."

"Stop it!" Choya grabbed her shoulders and gave her a vicious shake. It dissipated her anger to leave a freezing calm.

"I'm not becoming hysterical," she assured him.

He took a deep breath to control the anger she had aroused. "Do you think I liked what happened last night?"

A finely arched brow lifted. "I hope you aren't expecting me to apologize for my lack of encouragement."

"You know damn well that's not what I meant." His lips were compressed into a grim line, heightening the ruthless quality of his features.

"What did you mean?" Jacquie challenged. "Are you trying to deny that your intention was to seduce me? Pay the fiddler, as you call it. And you are the master fiddler, aren't you?"

"I am not here to apologize for what I didn't do."

"If you didn't come here for that, then you must have had another reason." She began tucking in her blouse again.

"You're impossible!" Choya declared savagely. His hand snaked out to check her movements, his harsh gaze almost unwillingly slipping to the exposed shadowy cleavage.

Jacquie emitted an exaggerated sigh and shook back her hair. "I wish you would explain why you're here."

"Why do you insist on making this difficult for me?" he snapped.

"Difficult for you?" she taunted. "What's the matter, Choya? Are you experiencing a few twinges of guilt and remorse for kidnapping me? Did you expect me to tell you it was all right and not to worry about it? Well, I can't and won't."

"I didn't expect you to," Choya replied tightly, a muscle twitching along his jaw.

Jacquie derived satisfaction from his growing anger. "Didn't you? I'll bet you expected me to let you force yourself on me. Isn't that how you were going to get the money for the repair bill on my car?"

"Will you stop it?" His voice trembled low and harsh.

"Why?" She rounded her eyes. "Are you planning to let me go? I hope not. I'd like Robbie to know what kind of a father he has before I leave."

"You leave Robbie out of this!" His fingers dug punishingly into the soft flesh of her upper arms as he jerked her against him, close to his glowering features.

"Why?" Jacquie didn't flinch from the fury in his eyes nor attempt to struggle from his grip. "He's been the cause of this from the beginning. He's the reason we saw each other after the accident. Because I have hair the color of moonbeams trapped in a mountain pool." She mocked him with his own description. "Did you think about your wife last night?"

"No!"

"You once said that I was trouble, but you've only had a taste of how much trouble I can be," she threatened.

"I'm warning you to leave my son out of this," Choya stated ominously.

"I'll tell you what," she murmured confidently. "If you let me go, then I'll leave Robbie alone."

"Do you think I'm not tempted?" he snarled, tightening his grip on her arms.

Jacquie tipped her head, the silken curtain of her hair swinging to the side and brushing against his sun-browned fingers. "I don't know."

Choya released her abruptly as if the feather softness of her hair against his skin was a match flame. His jaw was clenched. A fiery yellow gleam was in his eyes. He pivoted sharply and walked from the room with long impatient strides.

When the outside door slammed shut, Jacquie sank limply onto the bed. Her taunting words had been a means of revenge, but they left a bitter taste in her mouth. The throbbing ache in her heart hadn't eased. No satisfaction had been gained from making him angry with her accusations and threats, only more hurt. The unexpected discovery confused her.

PREVIOUSLY JACQUIE had avoided Choya. During the next few days, it was he who avoided her. Every time he was in a room with her or sat down at the table to share a meal, she could sense that he found her presence an irritant. Yet it was more than that.

When circumstances forced them to be together, his gaze rarely left her, but the gold mask never allowed her to see what he was thinking. He didn't come near her or indicate that he desired to touch her again.

Her relief was genuine. Yet, perversely, there were times when she would glance at him and remember the exciting caress of his hands and the mastery of his kiss. Then she would grow hot all over and have to excuse herself from the table or the room to escape his alert gaze and rid her mind of its wayward thoughts.

On Saturday, Robbie claimed her company. He conducted Jacquie on a grand tour of the ranch yard and his favorite places to play. The last stop was the barn. The shadowy darkness was a welcome change from the glare of the sun.

"I come here a lot," he informed her, his crutches clumping through the scattered pieces of old straw on the cement walkway. "There are a lot of neat places to play. I even have a secret hiding place in here." He darted her an uneasy sideways glance an instant after he had said that. "I'd like to show it to you, but—" he frowned.

Jacquie guessed the reason for his obvious dilemma. "If you showed it to me, it wouldn't be a secret place anymore," she reasoned.

"You don't mind, then?" Robbie breathed anxiously.

"Of course, I don't," she smiled.

"Come on." He started off again. "I'll show you my horse, Apache."

A gentle-eyed palomino leaned his head over a manger, whinnying at the small boy who approached. It was a small horse, a little over fourteen hands, the perfect size for a growing boy.

"You can ride him if you want," Robbie offered as he stroked the velvet nose thrust toward him. "He won't throw you or anything like that. Dad says he doesn't have any bad manners."

Jacquie stroked the sleek neck. "Thanks, Robbie, but I'm afraid I don't know anything about saddling a horse. Maybe another time."

"I can show you," he assured her hopefully.

"Why don't we wait until you can ride, too?" Jacquie suggested.

"That will be too long," he protested.

"Can you ride, Miss Grey?"

At the sound of Choya's voice, Jacquie pivoted sharply. Her sudden movement startled the palomino, metal hooves scraping through the straw bed to the concrete floor as he backed hurriedly away from the manger.

With the same cat quietness that had enabled him to enter the barn unheard, Choya walked toward them. His tawny gaze inspected her expression of wary alarm.

"I can ride fairly well," she replied. Abstractedly she was amused that he had addressed her so formally.

"I told her she could ride Apache," Robbie inserted.

Choya glanced down at the boy. "Why don't we let her ride Johnnycake instead?"

"What's that? The most vicious horse in the stable?" she accused, her anger surfacing with a sudden rush.

"Johnny?" Robbie questioned with a hooting laugh, missing the venom in her tone. Choya didn't as he surveyed her coldly. "He's real gentle, Jacquie." He glanced at his father. "She doesn't know how to saddle a horse, Dad. I was going to show her."

"Would you like to learn?" he challenged.

Jacquie hesitated. She wanted to do nothing that would bring her into prolonged contact with Choya. It had been several days since she had thought about escaping. But if she changed her mind, then a horse was the only easily accessible means of transportation.

"Yes, I would," she agreed.

"I'll get Johnny out of the corral, Rob," Choya glanced briefly at his son, "while you show her where the tack is."

With the gear collected, they met Choya at the corral fence. He didn't show her how it was done. He told her how to saddle and bridle a horse. His instructions were clear and concise and Jacquie discovered it wasn't as difficult as she had thought.

When the buckskin was saddled, Jacquie mounted and rode him around the yard. He was considerably more tractable than some of the stable horses she had ridden. She was brimming with confidence when she cantered him back to the barn.

Her smile faded as Choya caught at the bridle and stopped the buckskin beside him. "You're welcome to ride him whenever you like," he told her briskly. "But don't leave the yard unless someone is with you."

"Are you afraid I'll keep riding and forget to come back?" Jacquie taunted.

"That would be a dangerous thing to do," he replied grimly.

"Oh, I know you would come after me." Her mouth twisted bitterly.

"The danger is being alone in the desert."

"Is it?" she mocked, and slid from the saddle.

"He's a good horse, isn't he?" Robbie thumped forward.

"Yes, he is," Jacquie agreed, directing her attention to unsaddling the horse.

Robbie rested his weight contentedly on the crutches and watched her.

"Aren't you glad you're staying here with us?" he beamed.

She flashed a glittering look at Choya. "It's certainly been an experience."

The line of his jaw tightened ominously at her innuendo. He shoved the reins into Robbie's hand and walked away with a muttered comment that he had other things to do. His abrupt departure seemed to take the sting out of her resentment. Her gaze followed the wide shoulders, a hint of melancholy in its jewel depths.

On Sunday, Jacquie rode again, keeping to Choya's edict to stay close to the house. Her ride on Monday was longer, a reconnaissance tour of the land surrounding the ranch yard. The following day her previously unused muscles began voicing a vigorous protest at the exercise.

A hot shower that night had eased much of their stiffness, but they still ached with uncomfortable soreness. Sleep promised to be an elusive thing and Jacquie tied the robe sash around her waist and walked into the kitchen. A cup of hot chocolate before going to bed might help.

The flavored milk was just coming to a boil when the back door slammed. Jacquie tensed, knowing it had to be Choya since he had been out earlier nursing a sick bull. She had thought he had come back in already, but his appearance in the kitchen proved that the supposition had been wrong.

Her heart turned over at the sight of him so tall and vital, despite the lines of weary concern etched around his grim mouth. She turned quickly back to the stove, trying to hide the clamoring reaction of her senses to his masculinity.

"I'm fixing some hot chocolate. Would you like a cup?" she offered stiffly.

"Yes." He walked to the cupboard, removed a mug and set it on the counter near Jacquie. His gaze impatiently raked her length. "Don't you ever wear anything under your clothes?" he snapped.

Jacquie colored, keeping her gaze riveted to the pan on the burner. "I've just showered," she answered defensively. The searing memory of their previous encounter rushed forward with all its vividness.

A chair leg scraped the floor as Choya savagely yanked it away from the table. "Save it, Jacquie. I'm not in the mood to argue."

"Really?" she mocked.

"I've had a long day and I'm tired." He drew the words out through a tightly clenched jaw.

"Do you have a headache?" Jacquie taunted. "I thought that was a woman's excuse."

She poured an equal amount of cocoa into each cup and carried them to the table. Choya was standing beside the chair, his hand gripping the back, a trace of white around his knuckles. Her breathing changed to a quick, uneven rate. She set the cups on the table and reached shakily for a chair.

"Are you trying to provoke me into making love to you again?" he accused in a voice that was harshly soft.

Her head jerked toward him. "No!" she gasped the denial.

Frozen by the mesmerizing quality in his narrowed tawny gaze, she didn't resist when his hands closed over her arms and drew her toward him. The descending mouth tipped back her head, automatically arching her body toward him. The warmth of his kiss melted her bones, making her flesh pliant against the hardness of his length.

For so many days, Jacquie had felt empty inside. Now that hunger was being fed by Choya's hard embrace. Greedily she parted her lips to receive more, and his kiss deepened with satisfying passion.

A tanned hand slid up her shoulder to push aside the collar of her robe. His mouth began a sensual exploration of the exposed hollow of her throat. The wild song singing through her veins suddenly became a familiar tune—and she remembered with searing clarity when she had heard the notes before.

Her hands lifted to strain against his chest, twisting her body to elude the exquisite caress of his lips. "Please, let me go, Choya," she begged while she still had sufficient control to protest.

Smoothly he swung her off her feet into the cradle of his arms. The smoldering gold of his eyes burned over her face. Her heart skipped a beat, then accelerated madly at the promise of possession in their depths.

"You can't seem to make up your mind, can you?" His voice caressed her in a husky murmur. "I'll help you decide."

And he carried her out of the kitchen to her opened bedroom door. For an instant she was too overwhelmed by his mastery to struggle, then at the sight of the turned-down covers of her bed, her resolve came back. "Put me down, you low, contemptible beast!" she hissed. "That's what you are—an animal!"

Choya laughed and set her down without releasing her. His gaze moved suggestively over her rigidly erect form, almost physically touching her curves.

"You don't mean that," he smiled crookedly. "Don't pretend to be unwilling. You've already revealed otherwise."

"I loathe, hate and despise you!" Jacquie tried to pull free of his grip. "I can't stand to have you touch me. It's disgusting."

"It's strange that you don't show the way you supposedly feel," Choya mocked.

"What do you expect me to do?" she cried desperately. "I want to leave! I want to get away—and you won't let me go! You keep on insisting that you must be paid. And the only way you'll let me pay is—like this! I try to do what you want, but I can't. I can't!"

The sardonic glitter left his gaze as he studied her intently. He seemed to hesitate, testing her words and expression to see how much truth they contained.

The angry glitter of proud tears shimmered in her turquoise green eyes. "Isn't there some other way I can repay you?" she demanded in a choked voice. "Must you degrade me further?"

A frown creased his forehead. He released her wrist to brush corn silk hair from her cheek. Jacquie drew back from his touch, leaving his hand suspended in midair.

"It was never my intention to degrade you," he said quietly, letting his hand fall to his side.

"Wasn't it?" Disbelief silently accusing him of lying.

"Believe me, Jacquie, I never intended to hurt you." One corner of his strong mouth lifted in a brief, self-deprecating smile. "I thought you were harder. I never guessed it was a brittle mask of sophistication that gave you that appearance. If I'd known, I would never have voiced the terms of payment to you."

"Now that you do, I suppose you feel the damage is done and why should I object?" she taunted sarcastically.

"No!" he denied harshly. "I don't think that. Tonight I believed that you—" He clamped his mouth tightly shut, paused for an instant, then spoke more calmly. "I won't bother you anymore."

"Then let me go!"

Choya held her proudly demanding gaze for a long, hard moment, then, pivoting, he walked from the room without giving her an answer.

AFTER A restless night's sleep, Jacquie awakened to the strident buzz of the alarm clock. She dressed swiftly, wondering all the while if Choya would hand her the car keys this morning and tell her she was free to leave.

There was no sign of him in the kitchen. Jacquie hesitated at the hall leading to the living room. Perhaps she should find him to see if he had made a decision. On second thought, she would rather have him come to her. There was no need to beg for her freedom.

In a few minutes, Robbie would be coming for breakfast. As she started to fix it, she thought sadly of his reaction when he learned that she would be leaving. Not that she intended to tell him this morning.

Jacquie wasn't even certain that she would be leaving immediately. But after what Choya had said last night, she couldn't think of a single reason why he should force her to stay.

The food was on the table. Jacquie, Robbie, and Sam Barnett were all sitting down and eating when Choya came in from morning chores. His encompassing good-morning nod told her nothing. She tried to ease the anxiety of waiting with the reminder that he would probably want to speak to her alone before letting the others know.

"Dad—" Robbie paused as he finished spreading peanut butter over his toast "—can we go to Fort Bowie this Saturday?"

"I don't think so," Choya replied.

Robbie grimaced. "But you promised to take Gramps and me this summer, and it's already September. Summer is over."

"I made the promise before you broke your leg," came the firm reminder.

"So?" Pale brown eyes looked at Choya blankly.

"So you can't very well go with a cast on your leg," he explained patiently.

"I can go anywhere on my crutches," Robbie asserted. "Up and downstairs and all over."

There was a dubious shake of the dark head. "It's over a mile walk to the fort over some pretty rough terrain."

"We can make it, can't we, Gramps?" Robbie turned to Sam for confirmation.

"Eventually," the older man agreed with wry humor, "if we had all day."

"We could go all day." Robbie seized on his grandfather's words. "Jacquie could pack us a lunch and come along. We could all have a picnic together. Please, Dad?"

"We'll see." Choya lifted a coffee cup to his mouth, avoiding a direct answer.

"What's there to see about?" Robbie wanted to know.

"Where is this Fort Bowie?" Jacquie asked when Choya flashed his son an impatient glance.

"At Apache Pass," Robbie answered, forgetting his argument with his father for an instant.

"It's the ruins of the adobe fort built back when Cochise was making his raids," Sam Barnett explained. "It was to protect the settlers and traders going through Apache Pass. Later it was the main base during Geronimo's War. When he surrendered, the fort was abandoned. Now it's a National Historic Site."

"I bet there's lots of neat arrowheads and junk," Robbie declared. "Can we go, Dad?"

"Don't keep pestering your father," Sam Barnett warned. "He's just as like to tell you that you can't go 'cause you asked him so many times."

"But Jacquie wants to go, don't you, Jacquie?" The corners of his mouth sulked downward. "She's never been there before and neither have I for years and years."

"You aren't that old," Choya answered dryly. "Between now and Saturday I'll think about the trip. But don't keep asking me if we're going or I might do just what Gramps said."

"Ah, gee!" Robbie grumbled, and dunked his toast into a glass of milk.

"How'd that bull look this mornin'?" Sam asked.

"Better. You'd better check on him a couple of times this morning," Choya suggested.

"Where are you goin'?" Sam glanced up in surprise.

The tawny gaze slid briefly to Jacquie. She held her breath, wondering if he intended taking her into town and seeing her on her way out of it.

"To check the north fence," he answered, and set the empty cup back on the table.

Her hopes sank as Choya rose from the table. Why was he making her stay here? What did he hope to gain? Surely he didn't think she wanted to be here?

Confusion clouded her eyes as she watched him walk toward the small hallway leading to the back door. With a determined thrust of her chin, she decided she wasn't going to leave it alone.

Quickly she pushed her chair away from the table and followed him. He was nearly at the screen door when she entered the hall, her lighter footsteps drowned by the firm tread of his.

"Choya?" she called.

He paused, one hand holding the screen door ajar as he waited for her to reach him. His aloof gaze read the unvoiced question in her eyes.

"I won't be back for lunch," he said, and walked out of the door, again avoiding an answer.

Jacquie stared hopelessly after him.

CHAPTER NINE

PERCHED ON top of the corral fence, Jacquie munched an apple. The buckskin was waiting patiently for his share, nostrils flared, inhaling the scent in anticipation. Sighing, she handed him the core, absently ruffling his black forehead.

After two days, she was no closer to discovering what Choya's plans were. There was an unshakable sensation that to stay here much longer would be disastrous. The more she tried to ignore the feeling the stronger it became.

Restless and uneasy, she hopped down from the fence into the corral, wiping her palms on the tan denim of her slacks. She grabbed hold of the buckskin's halter and led him through the door into the barn, then she saddled and bridled the docile horse and was ready to lead outdoors to mount up.

She stopped and looped the reins over a stall board. There would be no more waiting: the decision was made in a split second. She wouldn't remain a prisoner on this ranch another minute. She left the buckskin tied in the stall and hurried into the house.

Working silently to avoid wakening the sleeping Sam Barnett, she stuffed a few essentials into a pillowcase. She didn't have any choice except to leave most of her things behind. It was impossible to carry them all on horseback. She would have to risk sending for them later—surely Choya wouldn't want to keep them. Her clothes certainly wouldn't be of any use to him.

Hesitating in the kitchen, Jacquie considered packing a lunch. It was nearly afternoon now and by nightfall she would reach some type of habitation. Besides, it would waste time. The longer she lingered here, the more risk she took that her plan might be discovered, either by Sam Barnett or Choya's unexpected return.

Astride the buckskin with the pillowcase tied by a string to the saddle horn, she had to make another decision—which way to go. The most direct route would be to follow the rutted lane to the graveled road and onto the highway. It was also the direction Choya would expect her to take, and the flat landscape would enable her to be seen at long distances.

Reining the horse away from the lane, Jacquie touched a heel to its flank and set off at right angles to the track. Once she was out of sight of the ranch house, and a considerable distance from the lane, she would turn and parallel its direction and not be in sight of anyone on the lane. It was a bold plan that just might work.

Because of the far-seeing distances of the desert, Jacquie rode at a trot for almost two hours before she completely lost sight of the ranch buildings. Her angle of flight had taken her into the foothills of the Dragoons.

An animal trail branched off to the right, a parallel line with the ranch lane. For the time being at least, she decided to follow it. If the trail turned into the mountains, she would abandon it.

Although the trail wound and twisted, dipped and climbed, it maintained the general direction that Jacquie wanted to take. The problem was that time was going by and she wasn't covering as much ground as she had thought she would. The rocky terrain and her limited horsemanship forced her to keep the buckskin at a walk.

Concerned about the sinking sun, she absently blamed the buckskin's uneven gait on the broken path. When they reached a smooth stretch of sand, it didn't alter, and glancing down, she saw he was favoring his right front leg. She stopped him and dismounted, cursing her rotten luck.

With her hands on her hips, she studied the surrounding land. She had accomplished one of the goals she had set out to do. She was away from the ranch and had avoided the well-traveled lane. There wasn't anyone in sight and not a sign of a building. And she was on foot with a lame horse.

"Come on, Johnny," Jacquie sighed heavily and took a short hold of the reins. "We certainly can't stay here."

Leading the limping buckskin, she continued on the narrow trail. The first dryness of thirst was in her throat, and the hollowness of coming hunger was in her stomach. She was beginning to realize just how foolish she had been. She had packed no food and carried no canteen of water.

When she had first come to the ranch, she had recognized the danger the mountain desert held for the unwary novice. During the last ten days, she had become familiar with the unending ruggedness of the landscape, but with that familiarity had come a subconscious contempt for its silent warning. What retribution would the desert exact for her foolishness?

The trail forked. The one to the left wound around a hillock toward the mountains; the right one continued in the general direction Jacquie thought she should take. But when she started on to the latter, the buckskin balked.

Jacquie took a firmer grip on the reins and tugged. "Come on, feller," she coaxed, but he refused.

The instant she relaxed the pulling pressure, the horse shifted toward the other trail. Crooning to him softly, she tried to persuade him to change his mind without success.

Straightening his black forelock, she murmured, "Do you know something that I don't know?" She tried again to lead him along the right fork and again the buckskin refused.

Giving up, she started up the left fork and the horse willingly followed. The twisted, curving trail climbed up into the edges of the mountain. Rarely was Jacquie able to see beyond the next turn. She had no idea where she was going; she just hoped the horse did.

A large boulder forced the trail to bend around it, and on the other side, Jacquie stopped in surprise. Nestled in a pocket of the mountain slope was a sparkling pool of water, shaded on three sides by rising rock walls. The horse shouldered her forward.

Tracks of various animals were around the small pool. Tufts of green grass grew near its edges. Jacquie watched the buckskin drink deeply from the waters before she knelt to scoop a small handful to her mouth. It was cool and sweet and wonderfully refreshing.

When she had satisfied her thirst, she sat down by one of the walled sides, leaning against the rock face. The buckskin limped to the grass, his teeth tearing at the green growth. Now she at least had water.

The western sky was on fire. The slipping yellow orb of the sun was crimsoning the world with streaks of red and flame orange. Clouds purpled under its light while the desert land reflected its burning glow. Jacquie had witnessed this sunset spectacle before. The cool stillness of approaching night had already invaded the land. Darkness would steal in quietly when the sun dipped below the horizon.

To leave the mountain pool when night was creeping in would be foolish. Here she had water and the horse had food even if she didn't. She concentrated on the beauty of the sunset and tried not to think about the empty growling of her stomach.

She glanced at her wristwatch, and knew that Choya was out looking for her. Possibly she had been missed as early as three hours ago. She wished he would find her, but there was little chance he would, at least not before nightfall. He would search the lane and road first. He wouldn't suspect that she had come in this direction.

Lavender hues dominated the sky. It was twilight. The evening star twinkled dimly. Jacquie shivered at the chill in the air and hugged her arms around her middle. It would be cold tonight and her thin blouse wouldn't offer much protection.

The buckskin lifted its head, its ears pricked toward the trail. Jacquie looked and saw nothing, but she could hear movement. She tensed. This was probably the only watering hole for miles. Maybe it was a wild animal coming for a drink. The buckskin's sides heaved in a searching whinny.

His call was answered by the whicker of another horse, then Jacquie heard the creak of saddle leather. It had to be Choya. Hastily she scrambled to her feet, her heart thumping wildly against her ribs. Not more than five minutes ago she had been wishing he would find her. Now she was looking for somewhere to hide.

He rounded the boulder and heat stained her cheeks. The sorrel horse was halted and Choya sat silently in the saddle, his unwavering gaze locked on to hers, his tawny eyes piercing like a golden arrow. Then his gaze shifted to the buckskin.

"Don't say it," Jacquie muttered angrily when its sharpness was returned to her. "I know it's called horse stealing."

"Were you trying to commit suicide?" His voice rolled out low, like thunder. "No food, no water, and obviously no matches or you would have a fire."

She tossed her head back in a gesture of defiance. "I was trying to get away from you. I didn't plan on spending a night in the desert," she retorted. "How did you find me?"

Choya swung effortlessly from the saddle. "A horse leaves tracks. I followed them."

"You wouldn't have found me," Jacquie declared bitterly. "I would have been far away from here if Johnny hadn't gone lame."

Dropping the sorrel's reins to the ground, Choya walked to the buckskin and ran an exploring hand over the right front leg. Lifting his hoof, he reached into his pocket and took out something that looked like a knife. There was a scraping sound, then he released the hoof and the buckskin stood squarely on all four feet.

"There was a stone in his shoe," he told Jacquie.

"That's all?" She stared at him in disbelief. "That's what made him limp? He isn't really hurt?"

"I imagine his foot is a little sore right now," Choya conceded. "Nothing worse than a slight bruise."

If only she had known what was wrong, she could have been miles away. Her ignorance aroused self-anger, followed swiftly by self-pity.

She stared at her captor, tall and dark as he walked toward her. The half-light of dusk threw his angular features in sharp relief, accenting their unrelenting hardness and the ruthless line of his mouth. He walked past her to the sorrel and pulled a rifle off the saddle scabbard.

Her turquoise eyes widened. "What are you doing?"

Choya cocked the rifle and pointed it into the air. He fired two shots fairly close together, paused and fired a third, then he returned his rifle to the scabbard, and glanced at Jacquie.

"I signaled Sam that I found you," he explained tersely.

"Can he hear that?" she frowned, wondering if he was closer to the house than she had thought.

"Sound, especially a rifle shot, carries a long way in this country." He moved to the leather pouches tied behind the saddle.

Her chin trembled. "I suppose you're going to make me go back with you," she said stiffly.

Unfastening one side of the pouch, Choya glanced at the facing golden light of the western horizon. "Not now. The trail is too difficult to follow in the dark."

"Do you mean we have to stay here all night?" Jacquie breathed with alarm.

"That's exactly what I mean." He removed a packet of sandwiches from the saddle bag and tossed it to her. "You might as well eat while I start a fire."

His grimness as he began gathering sticks from the surrounding brush bordered on a kind of anger that Jacquie found difficult to fathom. It increased the apprehension flowing through her veins. Each passing minute added to the electrically charged tension that tightened around her.

Despite her hunger, she could only eat one sandwich. She set the rest aside for Choya. A small camp fire was crackling as night drew its curtain over the sunset.

With the fire started, he unsaddled the buckskin, laying the saddle and blanket near Jacquie. Taking the lariat from his saddle horn, he strung a picket line for both horses, then unsaddled his own.

His continued silence was unnerving. Mockery and threats she could have combated, but this building tension scraped at her frayed nerves. When he set his saddle on the ground near hers, her control snapped.

"Let me go, Choya." Her voice trembled hoarsely in a demanding plea. "You can't really want to keep me prisoner anymore. What's the use of it?"

His jaw tightened forbiddingly, but he didn't look at her. The saddlebags were draped over his shoulder. He swung them down and opened one flap, towering above her, a dark silhouette against the camp fire. He removed a small square object and held it out to her.

"This is yours," he said gruffly.

Fighting tears of frustration that he had failed again to even reply to her demand, Jacquie rose to her feet. Impatiently she took the object he held out to her. Her lips parted to forcefully repeat the demand, but nothing came out as the familiar shape of the object claimed her attention.

She gazed at it in disbelief. "It's m-my wallet!" she breathed.

"Yes," was the low response.

Hurriedly she opened it. Nothing was missing. It was intact. "My money—it's all here." She raised her head, trying to see his face in the flickering firelight. "Where did you get it?" Then a chilling thought struck her. "You had it all the time, didn't you?" she accused.

"No!" Choya snapped, and breathed in deeply, almost angrily. "I didn't," he added in a voice leashed in anger.

Something in his tone made Jacquie doubt his answer. "Then where did it come from?" she challenged. "How did you get it?"

"From Robbie."

"Robbie?" she echoed the boy's name in shock. "How did he get it?"

"The day you spilled your purse on the sidewalk, he stuck the wallet inside his shirt," he explained grimly. "He didn't want you to leave, remember?" Jacquie remembered very well. "He decided if he took your wallet you wouldn't have any money to buy gasoline for your car."

"Let alone pay the repairs," she added with a short laugh that was bitter with irony. "And Robbie's had it all this time!"

"He's been keeping it in his secret hiding place in the barn."

She raked a weary hand through the side of her long hair, flipping it back to stream moon gold over her shoulders. "No wonder he didn't want to show me where his hiding place was," she murmured. Tears shimmered jewel bright in her eyes. "What made him decide to give it to you?"

"When I came back to the ranch this afternoon and discovered you were gone, Robbie was half-crazy with fear that you were hurt or lost. It never occurred to him that you'd run away," Choya stated. "In his childlike logic, he decided that if he gave back the wallet, I would find you safe and sound, otherwise something terrible would happen to you."

Acid tears burned down her cheeks. All of this happened to her because a little boy hadn't wanted her to leave him. His innocent taking of her wallet had precipitated the entire chain of events that had brought her to the ranch and finally to this mountain pool with Choya.

Dipping her chin, she closed her eyes briefly against the rush of pain.

Then she raised her head to gaze into his shadowed face.

"I have the money. Now will you let me go?" she demanded in a choked voice.

"You have every right to be angry," Choya began in harsh quietness.

"I'm not crying because I'm angry," Jacquie corrected, hiccoughing back a sob. "I'm crying because . . . just . . . because!"

The words brought a fresh flood of tears down her cheeks. Her shoulders shuddered with involuntary, silent sobs. Choya stood in front of her.

"Yes, I do know." The savageness in his tone was not directed at her.

He took a hesitant step forward. His hands closed lightly over her shoulders to draw her against him. Jacquie tried weakly to push him away, but racking sobs made her efforts puny. He gathered her close to his chest, rocking her gently in his arms.

Her cries were muffled by his shirt. Indifferently she was aware of the comforting hand stroking her silken hair. Strangely she realized that she was deriving solace from the embrace of the man who had hurt her. She clung to the man whose eyes were the color of a mountain cat's, feeling like a lost lamb being welcomed back to the fold.

His dark head bent near hers, and gently he kissed her tear-drenched lashes and wet cheeks. When his mouth found hers, it carried the salty taste of her own tears.

His kiss breathed warmth and strength into her. Under its reviving spell, life flowed back into her limbs. Her clinging hands wrapped themselves around his neck. But he disentangled them. Strong arms lowered her to the ground and a blanket was thrown over her.

"Go to sleep," Choya ordered.

The buckskin stamped the ground restlessly, as Jacquie watched him walk to the opposite side of the camp fire. She had paid the master fiddler. She had given him her heart.

HER LASHES fluttered. Something was wrong. There was no soft mattress beneath her. No pillow cushioned her head. There was only hard, uncomfortable ground beneath her and the chill of early-morning air around her. The memory of her futile attempt to flee from the ranch put the strange surroundings in perspective.

Jacquie opened her eyes, propping herself up on one elbow to search for Choya. She found him almost instantly over by the horses. Her frightened expression softened with love, then her muscles protested stiffly as she forced herself to her feet.

The buckskin was saddled and Choya was tightening the cinch on his sorrel. At her movement, he flicked a brief glance in her direction. The touch of his gaze was like a splash of cold water and she froze. The metal-

lic gold eyes had as much warmth in them as
the ashes of the dead camp fire. She shuddered uncontrollably.

"Good morning." His indifferent greeting
pierced her heart.

"Good morning," Jacquie returned stiffly.

With the reins of both horses in his hand, he
walked toward her. The boldly masculine features were drawn in an aloof expression.

He handed her the buckskin's reins.

"It's a long ride back," he stated briskly.
"We'd better get started."

"Yes," she agreed tightly, and mounted
quickly before he saw the agonizing pain in her
eyes.

As she pointed her horse toward the narrow
trail, Choya called her name. She halted the
buckskin and waited, her shoulders rigidly
squared. He reined his sorrel even with her
mount.

"Here." In his sun-browned hand was the
metal ring with her car keys. "You'll want to
leave when we get back to the ranch."

"Yes." In a stronger voice, she repeated the
agreement. "Yes, I will."

She shoved the keys in the pocket of her tan
slacks and kicked the buckskin's flanks, moving him out ahead of Choya.

Not another word was exchanged during the entire ride. The crushing silence ripped at her heart until it was in shreds by the time they reached the ranch yard. Her chin was quivering traitorously as she dismounted beside the corral. Unable to risk a glance at Choya, she dropped the reins and started for the house, leaving him to take care of the horses.

Robbie was racing across the yard toward her, using his crutches to catapult himself forward at a reckless pace. A grin of unbounded welcome was splitting his face from ear to ear. Sam Barnett was hobbling after him with his cane.

Paralyzed, Jacquie waited for Robbie to reach her. Her head pounded with dread, knowing how short-lived his happiness would be for her return. Choya's long strides were carrying him toward her.

"Jacquie! Jacquie! You're back!" Robbie cried in delight. When he would have hurled himself at her, Choya intercepted him, swinging him off his feet and straddling him on one hip. The boy readily transferred his affectionate greeting from Jacquie to his father. "You found her and brought her back, Dad! I knew you would! I just knew it!"

"Why aren't you in school?" Choya cast a sideways, frowning glance at Sam.

"I was waiting for Jacquie," Robbie beamed at her.

Sam shuffled forward, leaning heavily on his cane. "He refused to go until he'd seen Jacquie for himself. He was darned near makin' himself sick over it. There wasn't much else I could do but let him see she was all right," he said, giving the explanation that Choya had so silently demanded.

"I was afraid something would happen, and Jacquie and you wouldn't come back," Robbie added his fervent explanation to his grandfather's. His expression became suddenly apologetic. "I'm sorry about your billfold, Jacquie. I wasn't going to keep it, I was going to give it back to you. I only took it because I wanted you to stay."

"I know," she sighed, glancing helplessly at Choya's grim expression.

"Go up to the house, Jacquie," he ordered. His arm tightened around his son's waist. "I'll handle this." Jacquie opened her mouth, but nothing came out. She closed it, briefly meeting Sam's puzzled glance, and darted for the house. From her room, she could hear Robbie's protests at the news of her imminent departure, followed by his crying sobs. If only Robbie had been in school, she could have avoided this scene.

Without regard to neatness or order, she jammed her clothes and belongings into the suitcases. Inside, her heart was crying as tearfully as Robbie was. From her wallet, she took out enough money to cover the car repairs and the hotel bill. She slipped it under the alarm clock on her nightstand. When the last suitcase was filled, Choya appeared in the doorway of her room.

"Are you ready?" he asked.

Jacquie nodded, passing a hand across her face as if making certain no tears were on her cheeks. Choya picked up the two largest suitcases and juggled a third, leaving her to carry two small bags.

As she walked out of the room, she didn't pause for a last look. Whatever she might have left was left, and she didn't need a last glance to be able to remember the room and this ranch in the nights and months ahead.

When they walked outdoors, Robbie was huddled in a shadowy corner beneath the overhang. Jacquie looked at his bowed head with deep compassion and shared hurt. While Choya stowed her luggage in the back of her car, Sam limped forward. "I was just beginning to get used to having you around," he smiled wryly, and held out his hand. "Maybe

if you hung around for a while, you might
have learned how to cook."

Jacquie returned the smile weakly. "Thanks
for everything, Sam."

The elderly man nodded his rusty gray head
and stepped back. He glanced back toward the
house where Robbie was hunched in his ball of
misery.

"Aren't you going to come and say goodbye to Jacquie?" his grandfather called. His
question was met with silence. "You don't
want her to leave without saying goodbye, do
you, Robbie?" Sam called again. Nothing. He
glanced apologetically at Jacquie. "I'm sorry,
I don't know what's wrong with that boy's
manners. I'll go get him."

"No." She placed a hand on his arm to de-
tain him. "I...I understand how Robbie feels.
It's okay, really."

The last of her belongings were packed in
the car. Choya stepped away from the open
door. There was a lump in her throat as her
gaze ricocheted away from his impassive face.

The car keys were in her hand and the driver's door was open. But if Choya would say the
right words, Jacquie knew she would never
slide behind the wheel. He said nothing.
Moistening her lips, she stepped to the door.

"Jacquie!" It was Robbie who hurried toward her. "Jacquie, I don't want you to go!" He stopped in front of her, his face stained with tears and more were running down his cheeks. "I want you to stay!"

She knelt beside him. "I have to go, Robbie," she explained with a tight smile.

He hurled himself into her arms, wrapping his small hands around her neck to cling to her desperately. Jacquie hugged him, closing her eyes as the pain in her heart became unbearable.

"Please, don't go," he sobbed into her blouse. "Please, Jacquie!"

"I'm sorry," she whispered. Her mouth formed the words against his silky fine hair, almost the same shade of pale gold as her own.

"Please," he begged. "I love you. Please!"

A tear squeezed through her lashes, followed by another. "I love you, too, Robbie," Jacquie murmured, "but I have to leave."

"Why?" he pleaded to understand and clutched her tighter.

Jacquie knew if she had a hundred years, she would never be able to explain in a way he would understand. Opening her eyes, she focused her blurred vision on Choya, mutely appealing to him for help.

His gaze narrowed. He seemed about to say something, then the line of his mouth thinned tightly. Stepping forward, he gripped Robbie by the shoulders and drew him away from her.

"Goodbye," she whispered, but it was really said to Choya, not Robbie. She slid behind the wheel of the car before she completely lost control.

"You can't go!" Robbie started forward on his crutches, partially checked by the hard grip of his father's hands on his shoulders. "We're supposed to go to Fort Bowie on Saturday, Jacquie. You can't leave until after that."

"I can't stay until Saturday," she said, forcing an artificially bright smile. "I guess I'll have to see it some other time."

"You'll never find it by yourself," Robbie argued. "You've got to look through this pipe to find it and everything." She closed the car door and slipped the key into the ignition. "Don't go Jacquie. Please stay!"

There were too many unshed tears lodged in her throat for Jacquie to reply. Staring straight ahead, she started the motor. Robbie's cries were much too poignant for her to listen to many more without giving in. She didn't look back until she was driving down the lane. Then she glanced in her rearview mirror.

Robbie was hobbling after the car on his crutches. She could see that he was calling to her. Thank God she couldn't hear him. Soon she couldn't see him either as her eyes blurred with tears and the dust cloud from her accelerating car obscured him from view.

CHAPTER TEN

TIREDLY JACQUIE stepped from the car. She automatically walked to the side door of the two-story white house, stretching her shoulder muscles cramped from the long drive. The door was locked to morning visitors, but the scent of bacon frying was drifting through an open kitchen window. Jacquie knocked and waited.

A woman with light brown hair peered cautiously through the door's window. Her blue eyes rounded in a mixture of disbelief and delight. There was a momentary fumbling with the lock, then the door was thrown open and the screen door unhooked to admit Jacquie.

"Hello, mother," Jacquie managed before she was engulfed in her mother's embrace.

"Jacquie darling!" she exclaimed, a hand muffling her half-sob as she stepped back to look at her. "We've been so worried about you!" hugging her again. "Why didn't you call or write? I've hardly been able to live with your father, he's been so upset about you."

"I'm sorry, I—"

"Look at me!" her mother declared with a laughing sigh. "You've barely walked in the door and I'm already scolding you as if you were still a child. I'm glad you're back!"

"So am I." At this moment, Jacquie was glad to be back with her mother's arm curved warmly around her waist.

It wasn't Choya's, but she was going to have to get used to that.

"You look exhausted. Why don't you come sit down? I was just fixing breakfast for your father. Would you like some? Did you drive all night?"

"Yes to everything," Jacquie laughed at her mother's tumbling questions.

Her mother paused and laughed, her eyes twinkling brightly. "I've forgotten the questions."

"What's all this commotion about, Maureen?" Her father appeared at the doorway, adjusting his tie, silver hair glinting in the light. Jacquie looked at him lovingly, wondering how she could have forgotten how very handsome he was. He saw her and stopped. "Jacquie?" he breathed in a stunned voice.

The entire angry argument that had preceded her departure came rushing back. "Can I come home, Dad?" she asked humbly.

His mouth curved faintly with a smile, his chin quivering. He opened up his arms to her. "Welcome home, baby."

Jacquie flew into the bear hug of his arms with the same abandon that Robbie had once shown to her. "Oh, Dad, I'm so sorry about everything," she declared with a tiny sob.

"So am I." He kissed her soundly on the cheek. "Let's just forget about it."

Her smile was taut with emotion as he held her away. "You would be surprised how much you've learned, Dad, in the nearly three weeks I've been gone."

"I've got smarter, have I?" he teased. "That's a sure sign that my little girl has done some growing up."

"Quite a bit," Jacquie nodded.

"Sit down, you two," her mother instructed. "Breakfast is on the table." She started pouring the orange juice as they sat down at the small dinette table. "You can't have liked Los Angeles very well?"

"I didn't make it to Los Angeles." Jacquie sipped at her orange juice, carefully avoiding direct contact with the curious glances of her parents.

"Where have you been?" It was her father who asked.

"I made it as far as Tombstone, Arizona—The Town Too Tough to Die." She made a joke out of it. "I had a slight accident with the car—nothing serious," she hastened at her mother's quickly indrawn breath. "But I had to have it repaired before I could go on. Then I lost my wallet with all my money, identification, etcetera, and couldn't pay to get my car out of the shop."

"Is that when you called me?" Cameron Grey inquired with a tilt of his head. At Jacquie's silent nod, he sighed. "I was angry when you called. Your mother and I had just been arguing about the way I'd lost my temper before you left. I kicked myself a hundred times after you phoned for not finding out where you were."

"I understand. I was a bit frantic at the time, though," Jacquie smiled faintly.

"I expect you were," her mother declared. "Stranded with no money. What did you do?"

"I . . ." she hesitated. "I got a job."

"Doing what?" Her father glanced at her curiously.

Spreading jam on her toast turned into a project. "Keeping house and cooking for a local rancher."

"My little girl doing housework and cooking!" he laughed incredulously. "We should have been there, Maureen. That would have been a sight worth seeing!''

"Cam!" her mother cautioned.

"Dad's right." Jacquie wanted to keep the subject on a light note and avoid any questions that might become too probing. "It was quite a sight. Ch—Mr. Barnett had this monstrous antique stove for cooking. He referred to my meals as burnt offerings."

"What about his wife? Was he married?" Maureen Grey asked.

"No, he was a widower." She shifted quickly away from his marital status. "He had a little boy named Robbie. I wish you could have met him, mother. You would have fallen in love with him."

"It sounds like you did," her father commented at the warmth in her voice.

"I did," Jacquie admitted. She loved Robbie almost as much as she loved his father, although not in the same way. She bit into the slice of toast.

"It must have been a well-paying job for you to earn enough to pay the repairs on your car and have enough money to come home," her father observed.

Did she detect a note of suspicion in his voice? Or was it her own guilty conscience? Jacquie wasn't certain which it was.

"Actually my billfold was found with everything in it, money and all. But by that time I'd already decided that I wanted to come home," she explained, adding with a bright smile, "and here I am!"

"What are you going to do now?" Cameron Grey glanced up from his plate, eyeing her thoughtfully. "Do you still plan on getting a job and working?"

"I was hoping it wouldn't be too late to enroll for the fall term at the university," Jacquie answered.

"I thought college was a waste of time," he mocked her gently.

"It was when I didn't know how I wanted to put the education to use," she smiled, not offended nor angered by his needling of her past outbursts. "I think I might like to teach in the elementary levels. Maybe the first or second grade with children Robbie's age."

"My girl leaves a rebel and comes back a woman." He shook his silvery head in a marveling gesture. "I don't know if it's the rancher or who it is I have to thank for this change, but I'd certainly like to shake his hand some day."

Jacquie crimsoned a deep red. She couldn't help herself. His statement was the truth, but he had been speaking figuratively. She was a woman in love, not a schoolgirl turned rebel anymore.

"I couldn't have been that bad when I left," she laughed self-consciously, hoping neither of her observant parents would guess the reason for the blush.

"You were a bit of a handful, but not really so bad," her father smiled.

"That's good." She breathed in deeply. "Well, what have you two been doing while I've been gone?" she asked, diverting the conversation to another topic.

Her father left for his office directly after breakfast. Jacquie helped her mother clear the table, letting her do most of the talking. Together they unloaded the car, carrying the luggage to Jacquie's bedroom.

"Is something wrong, Jacquie?" Maureen Grey tipped her head to one side, only a few white hairs intermingling with her light brown hair.

"Wrong?" Jacquie tensed, smiling nervously. "What do you mean?"

"You seem…well…preoccupied, I guess," her mother frowned.

"I suppose I'm just tired from the long drive and lack of sleep," she shrugged.

"Of course you need rest and I've been chattering away like a magpie. We can finish unpacking later,'' her mother suggested. ''Meanwhile, you climb into bed and get some sleep. We have plenty of time to talk.''

''That's a marvelous idea,'' Jacquie agreed, suddenly feeling as tired as she had claimed to be. She gave her mother a quick hug. ''It's good to be home.''

Tears shimmered in the blue eyes. ''You have no idea how glad your father and I are to have you back. Now get some sleep.''

''I will,'' Jacquie promised.

THERE WAS the cool nip of November in the air. Jacquie gathered her college books and papers from the passenger seat and stepped from the car. Another night of studying was ahead of her, making up for the times when she had merely got by with the minimum of effort.

Plus, it was the only certain way she had to block out her potent memories of Choya. With each passing day they became more vivid. So far she hadn't confided in her parents about him, although she thought her mother suspected there was more to her story than Jacquie had told.

She entered the house through the side door into the kitchen.

''Mom, I'm home!'' Jacquie called.

Setting her books on the dinette table, she walked to the cupboard and removed a glass, then to the refrigerator where she filled it with cold milk. Her mother appeared in the doorway, a beaming smile on her attractive face.

"There's someone here to see you," she announced.

"Who?" Jacquie asked uninterestedly, raising the glass to her lips.

"A Mr. Barnett from Arizona. He said he met you there. I can't remember his first name. It was very unusual though."

Jacquie nearly choked on her milk. "Choya!"

"Yes, that's it," her mother nodded.

"What's he doing here? How did he know where I was?" Liquid fire raced through her veins at the thought that he was just in the next room. She panicked, knowing she didn't dare see him again.

"I suppose you gave him your address," her mother said. "He has obviously come just to see you."

"Tell him—" She rubbed her hand across her forehead, trying to force herself to think. "Tell him that I'm sorry, but I can't stay. I'm on my way to the library to do some research on a term paper. I've got to go now." Setting the glass on the counter, she rushed for her books on the table.

"Nonsense." Her mother tucked a hand beneath her elbow. "If he has made a special trip to stop to see you, the least you can do is to say hello."

"Mother, no, please!" Jacquie protested anxiously.

Maureen Grey stopped, frowning, "Why on earth are you so afraid to see the man?"

"I'm not afraid." The denial was an outright lie. "It's just that—" she began helplessly, then realized it was no use. She couldn't make her mother understand without explaining in detail. "I guess I have time," she sighed in defeat.

"That's more like it," her mother nodded. "He's in the living room waiting to see you."

Choya was standing in front of the sofa when Jacquie entered the living room with her mother. Tall and stunningly masculine, he wore a Western leisure suit of wheat tan with inserts of deep brown, matching the umber shade of his thickly waving hair.

Her stomach contracted sharply as the tawny cat eyes held her gaze with mesmerizing ease. Not for the first time Jacquie had the sensation she was looking at a predatory beast that had sighted its prey. The taut alertness was etched in every muscled inch of him. She felt weak at the knees.

"How are you, Jacquie?" The rich timbre of his voice tugged painfully at her heart.

"Fine." She swallowed convulsively. "And you?"

"Fine." He paused. "I promised Robbie I would see you while I was here."

So that was why he had come, Jacquie thought silently—to fulfill a promise to his son. The tiny hope that he might have wanted to see her for himself was dashed to the ground.

"Oh!" A light dawned in her mother's blue eyes. "You're the Mr. Barnett that Jacquie worked for when she was in Arizona."

"That's right." His gaze narrowed slightly on Jacquie before he nodded to her mother in acknowledgement.

"I appreciate your stopping by," Jacquie inserted stiffly. "I'm sorry I can't ask you to stay longer, but I have a great deal of work to do. I was on my way to the library when mother told me you were here."

"I see." Choya exhaled slowly and grimly.

"If you'd known Jacquie before she went to Arizona," her mother spoke up, "you wouldn't believe the way she's changed since she came back. It used to be her evenings were taken up with parties and activities. Now, it's studying. She rarely goes out anymore."

"Mother, please!" Jacquie murmured angrily, turning away from Choya's piercing glance.

"Would you mind, Mrs. Grey, if I spoke to your daughter alone for a few minutes?" he asked with grating deference.

"Of course not," she smiled, missing Jacquie's beseeching look to stay. "I have dinner to start anyway."

An electric silence filled the room when her mother left. The charged currents drained the color from her face and sent her blood pounding wildly in her ears. Jacquie walked shakily to the large picture window.

"How did you know where I was?" she tried to breach the silence.

"I contacted your insurance company and they gave me your parents' name and address here in Dallas," Choya answered. Jacquie had forgotten all about giving him the name of her insurance company when she had had the accident with his jeep. "I telephoned the other night to see if they knew where you were. I found out you were here."

Jacquie tipped her head back, gazing sightlessly at the sky. Vaguely she remembered her mother mentioning that some man had called for her the other night. It hadn't meant anything at the time. Although she hadn't gone out since she had come back, that hadn't stopped anyone from asking.

"Unfortunately I didn't know you were coming or I would have arranged not to be here," she said with bitter truthfulness.

"That's what I thought." His comment was clipped and harsh. At the sound of his approach, she turned warily to face him. "You left this behind."

Her gaze flicked briefly to the folded bills of paper money in his hand. She guessed it was the money she had left on the nightstand.

"It's yours. I always pay my debts in full!" she flashed.

A muscle leaped in his jaw. "I deserved that." Choya breathed in slowly, glancing at the money in his hand.

"You've explained how you found me. Now tell me why you're here," Jacquie challenged, reeling at his intoxicating closeness yet unable to make her trembling legs carry her a safe distance away.

Like a magnet, his tawny eyes seemed to draw her toward him. The enigmatic light in their depths tightened the muscles in her chest until she could hardly breathe.

"I came to take you back with me," he stated.

Her head jerked as if he had slapped her. "No!" she gasped in pain.

"Robbie misses you."

A wavering laugh broke from her throat. She turned back to the window, cradling her arms around her middle to ward off the sudden chill.

"I want you to come with me as my wife," Choya said firmly, leaving her in no doubt that he meant it.

"I like Robbie very much," she murmured in a choked voice. "But I want more out of life and a marriage than to be some little boy's stepmother."

His hands settled onto her shoulders, and she didn't have the strength to move away. She closed her eyes, reveling in the exquisite pain of his touch.

"I was wrong when I said you were trouble," his low whisper caressed her hair. "The trouble has been living without you, Jacqueline."

Exerting the slightest pressure, he turned her into his arms. Her turquoise eyes were riveted to his mouth, watching it form more enchantingly beautiful words.

"I've wanted to do this ever since you walked into the room," he murmured.

His fingers tangled themselves in the silken length of her silver blond hair. His mouth covered hers in a searching yet possessive kiss, and Jacquie responded to it with all the pent-up longing in her heart.

Then he was tearing his mouth away from her lips. The iron band of his arms held her so tightly she didn't think she could breathe, but she didn't care. She felt him shudder against her and the joy seared through her veins.

"Lord knows I never intended to fall in love with you," Choya muttered thickly against her hair. "After what I've done to you, it would be poetic justice if you hated me."

"You said Robbie missed me," Jacquie breathed, remembering the anguish when she had thought he only wanted her back for his son.

"He does, but not as much as I do. I can't sleep without remembering what it was like to have you in my arms and cuddle you against me like a sleeping kitten," he murmured. "I told myself I was only coming to see you to make sure you were all right. The minute I saw you I knew I had to take you home with me. I used Robbie as a reason because you love him."

"Not as much as I love his father," she whispered.

He lifted his head to gaze doubtingly into her upturned face. "Do you?"

"I love you, Choya." Her voice quaked with the depth of her love. "I have, I think, from the beginning. At first it was fascination. But later, it turned to love."

"Why didn't you tell me?" he groaned, raining kisses over her cheeks and throat as if trying to make up for all the hurt they had both been through.

"Why did you let me go? Why didn't you make me stay? I needed you," Jacquie quivered in his passionate embrace.

"I felt like the lowest animal on earth. I had no right to ask you to stay or to force you to stay." His low voice was laced with self-disgust. "Yet I couldn't make myself say the words that would set you free—not until I found out how Robbie was involved, and even then I couldn't let you go without holding you one last time. I'm warning you, Jacqueline, we Barnetts can be very ruthless to get what we want."

"Don't I know it!" she laughed, but this time without pain.

"You will marry me." It was half a question and half a command.

"Yes—"

Jacquie never had a chance to complete her answer as his mouth bruised hers, demanding an answer that was not verbal. Her arms slid around his shoulders, clinging to him.

The front door opened, and Cameron Grey walked in. He glanced at the embracing couple and halted in shock. It was several seconds before Choya bothered to lift his lips from Jacquie's.

Tawny eyes danced to the man standing just inside the door. His compelling features were radiant from the light that glowed in her turquoise green eyes.

"You must be Cameron Grey, Jacqueline's father." He removed one arm from around Jacquie, still holding her firmly against his chest with the other. He offered his hand to her stunned father. "I'm Choya Barnett. I'm going to marry your daughter and take her home to Arizona."

Her father blinked. "But she's just come back!"

"You've had her for twenty-one years." Choya smiled into her upturned face. "Now it's my turn. And I have the feeling that a lifetime together isn't going to be long enough."

HARLEQUIN®

my Valentine

1993

The most romantic day of the year is here! Escape into the exquisite
world of love with MY VALENTINE 1993. What better way to celebrate
Valentine's Day than with this very romantic, sensuous collection of four
original short stories, written by some of Harlequin's most popular
authors.

**ANNE STUART
JUDITH ARNOLD
ANNE McALLISTER
LINDA RANDALL WISDOM**

**THIS VALENTINE'S DAY, DISCOVER ROMANCE
WITH MY VALENTINE 1993**

Available in February wherever Harlequin Books are sold.   VAL93

HARLEQUIN PRESENTS®

A Year Down Under

Beginning in January 1993, some of Harlequin Presents's most exciting authors will join us as we celebrate the land down under by featuring one title per month set in Australia or New Zealand.

Intense, passionate romances, these stories will take you from the heart of the Australian outback to the wilds of New Zealand, from the sprawling cattle and sheep stations to the sophistication of cities like Sydney and Auckland.

Share the adventure—and the romance— of A Year Down Under!

Don't miss our first visit in
HEART OF THE OUTBACK by Emma Darcy, Harlequin Presents #1519, available in January wherever Harlequin Books are sold.   YDU-G